Trapped by Fire!

Danny and Mr. Matthews gazed out of Mr. Matthews's small plane. "It's the Professor," cried Danny. "See? He's on that rocky shelf. He's waving his handkerchief."

"I see him. There's Pippit, too. Sit tight. I'll try to fly in front of them so we can see what they're doing."

The two men were standing on a broad ledge to which they must have climbed to escape the fire. Behind them rose a wall of solid limestone. On one side the ledge dropped away into a wooded gorge from which flames were rising in places. On the other side, the shelf vanished into a haze of smoke.

"They're boxed in!" said Mr. Matthews.

Danny Dunn and the Heat Ray

**Jay Williams and
Raymond Abrashkin**

Illustrated by

Owen Kampen

AN ARCHWAY PAPERBACK
POCKET BOOKS • NEW YORK

POCKET BOOKS, a Simon & Schuster division of
GULF & WESTERN CORPORATION
1230 Avenue of the Americas, New York, N.Y. 10020

Published by arrangement with McGraw-Hill Book Company
Library of Congress Catalog Card Number: 62-14677

ISBN: 0-671-29969-7

First Pocket Books printing November, 1979

10 9 8 7 6 5 4 3 2 1

Trademarks registered in the United States and other countries.

Printed in the U.S.A.

The authors are grateful to Owen Kampen for aeronautical material; to William D. Feeny, Squadron Commander in the Civil Air Patrol, for much information and advice; and especially to John Atwood, Research Director of the Perkin-Elmer Corporation, for information about the laser and for allowing us to see it in operation.

This book is for the Siegel boys:
Jonathan
Andy
and Jeffrey Nahum

Contents

1
An Important Announcement

Washington Avenue was swarming with boys and girls on their way to school. They were as thick as ants streaming to an anthill, and their laughter and chatter, calls, whistles, and shouts made such a racket that Mr. Polseno, the candystore owner, looked nervously at the vibrating glass of his big window. Then he blinked and looked again.

A sturdy, freckled, redheaded boy was just passing in front of the window. And above his head dangled four school books bound together with a strap. They seemed to be floating in the air.

Mr. Polseno rubbed his eyes. As the boy moved, the books moved with him. The candystore owner ran to the door. Then he saw that the books were hanging from a large, silvery balloon some three feet in diameter, attached by a long cord to the boy's belt.

"Danny Dunn!" said Mr. Polseno. "Hey, boy, you nearly gave me heart failure. What are you, a secret Air Force weapon?"

"Oh, hello Mr. Polseno," Danny said cheerfully. "How do you like my new painless way of carrying books?"

"Very fine, unless a bird flies headfirst into it," said Mr. Polseno. "Where did you get such a big balloon? I didn't know they made them that size for kids."

"Oh, this isn't a toy," Danny replied. "It's used for sending weather instruments aloft. Professor Bullfinch was using some of them for his experiments, and he gave me one. They're filled with helium, you see, so they can lift quite a weight."

He jerked his thumb at a tall, thin sad-looking boy who had been walking with him. "I tried to convince Joe to use one, but he's nervous about them."

Joe Pearson, Danny's best friend, shook his head. "I'm just waiting for it to blow up, or fly off with all his books," he said. "Every time Danny tries one of these nutty experiments, there's some kind of trouble."

A pretty, blue-eyed girl with her dark hair in a long pony tail, was on the other side of Joe. Her name was Irene Miller and she lived next door to Danny. "Stop worrying, old Gloom," she laughed. "If I hadn't left my books in school yesterday, I'd have them floating up there, too. The only problem I can see in this experiment is what to do with the balloon when we get to school."

"No problem at all," Danny said airily. "I'll tie it to the bicycle rack outside."

"It'll probably fly off with the rack and all the bikes," said Joe. "Don't say I didn't warn you."

Mr. Polseno went back into his store, chuckling to himself, and the three young people walked on. As they turned into the school grounds, two boys who had been playing mumblety-peg stopped their game and stared.

One of them, a plump boy with curly black hair, said, "Look, Eddie—balloons! It's a parade."

Eddie Philips got up and dusted off the knees of his trousers. He was broad shouldered, with heavy, blond eyebrows that gave his face a sulky appearance.

"Hey, Danny," he called. "What happened? Did your head swell so much that it finally broke loose?"

Danny grinned. "What's the matter, Snitcher?" he retorted. "Are you jealous of scientific inventions?"

Eddie, who hated to be called "Snitcher," scowled. "Scientific inventions, eh? Like the time you blew out every light in the school demonstrating an electrical generator? What's so great about hanging your books on a balloon?"

"Oh, they must weigh about four pounds," Danny said cheerfully. "Doesn't your arm get tired carrying yours to school?"

"My arms don't get tired that easily," said Eddie. "What you should have up there is a little airplane instead of a toy balloon. That would be a real scientific achievement."

"Hmm," Danny said, looking interested. "That's not such a bad idea. Only, I don't know what would keep the plane up—"

Eddie guffawed. "How about that, George? The great expert, Danny Dunn, and he doesn't even know what keeps a plane up in the air!"

"Sure I do," Danny retorted. "It's—well—um—that wasn't what I meant," he finished, lamely. "I meant, how would you fuel a model plane so it would—"

But Eddie wasn't listening. "Go ahead," he jeered. "Tell us what keeps a plane up."

Dan scratched his head. He was deeply in-

"What you should have is a little airplane."

terested in science and knew more about some aspects of it than most young people did. His mother was housekeeper for the famous Professor Euclid Bullfinch, and the Professor had taught Danny a great deal about the marvels of the universe. It was hard for the boy to admit that he didn't know the answer to what ought to be a simple question for someone living in the twentieth century. But at last he said, "I— I guess I don't know. Do you, Irene?"

Irene shook her head. She shared Danny's interest in science and planned to become a physicist some day. But she had to say, "I guess it has something to do with its wings, but I don't know what."

Eddie said loftily, "Huh! So you don't know as much as you think you do. Anybody knows that a plane's engine is what makes it fly. The engine pulls the plane up and keeps it up by pulling it through the air. If the engine conks out, the plane falls, doesn't it?" He picked up his school books. "Come, George," he said, "let us leave these uncouth characters. They are little better than dopes."

The school bell began its shrilling at that moment. "We'd better run," Joe said. "We'll be late."

Danny quickly untied his books from the balloon. He trotted to the side door of the school and hitched the balloon cord to the bicycle rack which stood outside. As they went into the building, he said thoughtfully to his friends, "You know, I don't think Snitcher was right. A glider flies without an engine. So does a kite. It must be something else that holds a plane up."

He continued to wonder about the problem all during the morning periods. He thought about it during English, and when Mr. Green asked him who wrote *Hamlet,* he replied, "William Airplane." He was puzzling over it during Geometry, so that when he was asked to define a right triangle, he said, "A right triangle is one that flies without an engine." And in Science, when Miss Arnold said, "Danny, perhaps you can tell us what a proton is," he sat up straight, gave a laugh, and blurted, "Air, of course."

Miss Arnold looked a little startled, for Danny was one of her best pupils. "Air?" she said.

"Holds it up," said Danny. "Of course, that's it. But how?"

"How does air hold a proton up?" said Miss Arnold in bewilderment.

"Yes, that's the real question," Danny nodded.

"DANNY DUNN!" said Miss Arnold.

"That is *not* the question. I don't know where you've been, but you haven't been in this classroom. I don't want to have to talk to you again about daydreaming."

The rest of the class was giggling, and Danny's face burned. "Gosh, I'm sorry," he murmured.

Miss Arnold sighed, and glanced at her watch. "Well," she said, "as long as we've been stopped short, and it's nearly the end of the period, I'll make my announcement. I had planned to make it just before dismissal. I think all of you—including Mr. Dunn, if he can keep his mind on what I'm saying—will find this important. There is to be a State Science Fair for the students of all our schools. I am sure many of you will want to enter it with displays, models, and demonstrations."

There was a buzz of interest from the class. Irene raised her hand, and said, "Miss Arnold, when is to be held?"

"The week after Thanksgiving," Miss Arnold answered. "That gives you more than two months to prepare for it. There will be prizes for the best entries in each age group. And our own principal, Mr. Standish, is offering prizes for the best entries from this school. Now, I haven't any doubt that all the prizes are going to be snapped up by people from this class. I will be glad to help any of you with advice or suggestions for reading or reference. I know that many of you have special interests already, and I expect there will be some exciting variety."

Victoria Williams said, "Shall we tell our plans when we've decided on them, Miss Arnold? Or shall we keep them secret?"

Miss Arnold smiled. "It will be much more fun, I think," she said, "if the entries come as a surprise. However, we don't want duplications if we can help it. I think the best way to do it would be for each of you to let me know about your project as soon as you decide on it. I'll keep a list, and then if there's any doubt we can discuss whether you ought to go on with it or not. I hope you'll bring your projects to class as soon as you can. In fact, I'll invite Mr. Standish to come and see the first one that's brought in, and we can have it demonstrated for all of us."

The class was murmuring with excitement and anticipation. Irene turned round in her seat and said to Danny, "Isn't it terrific? Shall we do one together?"

"Sure," Danny replied. "And I think I've got a great idea."

Miss Arnold clapped her hands. "Very well, class. Come to order, please."

They slowly quieted, and she went on. "Now we have a few minutes left before the bell, so perhaps we can return to our discussion of the atom. I was just asking about—"

Her voice trailed away. She had been facing the windows, and she stood suddenly motionless with an odd look on her face.

"How extraordinary," she exclaimed. "I thought I saw—but that's impossible."

"I saw it too, Miss Arnold," cried Gordon Gianninoto, who sat next to the window. "It was a flying saucer."

His twin brother, Jamie, added, "It was a big round silvery thing, wasn't it? It flew right past the window."

Miss Arnold rubbed her forehead with her fingertips. "I don't understand," she said. "What on earth can it mean?"

Danny sighed. "I think I know, Miss Arnold," he said sadly. "It means I didn't tie a tight enough knot, and I'm going to have to carry my books home from school."

2
Heads or Tails

Right after school, Danny, Joe, and Irene held a meeting. Danny's room was on the top floor of Professor Bullfinch's house, and his window looked out over the back garden to the distant roofs and towers of Midston University. The room was crammed with books, shelves full of radio equipment, a microscope, a chemistry set, wires, magnifying glasses, tools, and a litter of old experiments and projects which Danny kept because he felt that their parts might come in handy some day. His mother continually tried to clean out the room, and Danny just as stubbornly refused to throw anything away, so that there was barely space for him and his two friends. They made themselves as snug as possible—Irene in the armchair, Joe

11

lounging on the bed, and Danny perched on the edge of the desk.

Danny said solemnly, "Flight."

"Okay," said Joe. "Who?"

"Who what?"

"Who are we going to fight?"

"*Flight*, knucklehead." Danny grinned. "My idea is to make a project based on what Snitcher said. I think it is very catchy, a swell slogan for a display."

"On what Snitcher said?" Joe repeated. "You mean, 'They are little better than dopes'? I don't think that's such a good slogan."

"No, Joe," Irene said patiently. "He means, 'What keeps a plane up.'"

"That's it," said Danny. "And I'm sure I've figured out the answer—anyway, part of it. It's air that holds up a plane, or a glider, or a kite."

"Sure," Joe nodded. "A remarkable deduction. Then why won't it hold me up? If I tried flapping my arms and jumping up in the air, I'd fall on my face."

"That's the part I don't understand," Danny confessed. "I don't know how it works, but I'll bet I'm right. I'm sure we can find out the answer. Then we can make a display showing how it works, maybe with a model airplane. What do you think, Irene?"

"Fine. I'd love to try."

"I'll letter your signs," Joe said, yawning. "But don't expect me to understand what's going on. Science is not my subject. Maybe I'll write a poem in praise of your prize—when you get it."

"Where shall we go first, to find the answer?" Irene asked.

"Oh, I've already figured that out, too," said Danny. "We'll consult an authority."

"You mean Professor Bullfinch?"

"Oh, no. I mean my mother."

"No kidding?" said Joe. "I'd never have guessed it."

"Guessed what?" asked Danny.

"That your mother was a flier."

"She's not a flier."

"Oh." Joe rubbed his chin. "Well, neither am I. So why not consult me? Then we won't have to walk all the way downstairs."

"My mother isn't a flier, but her cousin, Charles Matthews, is," Danny explained. "And," he added casually, 'I know she's baking brownies, so if we go downstairs—"

Joe was already halfway to the door.

When they came trooping into the kitchen, Mrs. Dunn sighed heavily. She pushed a lock of hair as red as Danny's out of her eyes and said, "I have always felt that children have a kind of sixth sense, a mysterious way of mind reading that tells them when something good has just come out of the oven. Now I know it.''

''Why, Mom?'' Danny said innocently. ''Have you just baked something?''

Mrs. Dunn took up a knife and began cutting into a pan of sweetly fragrant chocolate brownies. ''Sit down,'' she said. ''And try not to get crumbs all over my clean floor.''

''Well, actually, we came downstairs to ask you about something else,'' Danny said. ''But if you're going to *force* us to eat—''

''Delicious,'' Joe mumbled, with his mouth full.

''They're lovely,'' said Irene. ''Thank you, Mrs. Dunn.''

''You're the best cook in the world, Mom,'' Danny said.

''Oh, go on with you,'' said Mrs. Dunn, smiling. ''Now that you've flattered me, what was it you wanted?''

''We've got to do some research about flying,'' said Danny. ''I thought maybe we could go see your cousin, Mr. Matthews.''

''Well, that's easy enough. I'll call Charles right now, and see if he's home.''

Mrs. Dunn went to the phone. Joe cleared

his throat, and said, "While we're waiting, Mrs. Dunn—"

"Yes, you may have another brownie," said Mrs. Dunn, dialing the number.

Danny rested his chin on his palms and gazed at his friend. "Where do you get your appetite from?" he asked.

"I didn't get it from anywhere," said Joe. "It came with me. Do you want those crumbs on your plate?"

Mrs. Dunn returned from telephoning with a slip of paper. "Here's my cousin's address," she said. "He lives on Myrtle Street, on the other side of the university. Jane—his wife— said he's due home in a little while, but you can go over now and wait for him."

Danny jumped to his feet. "Thanks, Mom," he said. "Come on, Irene. Joe, you can bring the crumbs with you. Let's go."

"Danny, dinner is at six," Mrs. Dunn called, as they ran out the back door.

Mrs. Matthews, a slender, pretty woman, had just finished baking ginger cookies. She sat the three friends around the kitchen table and put a plateful in front of them. Joe sighed happily.

"What a beautiful day this has been," he said. "Whom else shall we visit?"

Mr. Matthews was tall and rawboned. He came home a few minutes after they had arrived, and shook hands with the young people with a rather mournful, absent-minded air which reminded Danny of Joe.

"No cookies left for me?" he said. "No, don't offer me one. They're bad for my digestion." He picked up a cookie, looked at it sadly, and bit into it. "I can't resist them," he added. "This one will probably kill me. How's your mother, Dan?"

"Fine, sir."

Irene watched Mr. Matthews pick up another cookie. "Oh, my," she said, worriedly, "maybe you shouldn't eat that one."

"There isn't a thing wrong with his digestion, dear," said Mrs. Matthews. "He's just the tragic type."

"We came over," Danny said, "because we want to find out what makes a plane fly."

"The pilot," said Mr. Matthews promptly.

Irene giggled. Danny said, "No, I mean we want to learn what keeps it up in the air. You see, we're planning a demonstration for a science fair."

"Yes," Mr. Matthews said gloomily, "it's a question I often ask myself. I'll be flying along up there, and suddenly I say to myself, 'What's holding this crate up?' " Then, abruptly, he grinned. "I'm only joking," he said, clapping Danny on the shoulder. "I'll be glad

to help you. Only, I haven't the time right now. I'm a member of the C.A.P.—the Civil Air Patrol, you know—and I've got to go over to the airfield this afternoon. I'm afraid I have to leave right now."

The three looked disappointed at this, but he went on. "Tomorrow is Saturday, isn't it? I'll be flying a fire patrol tomorrow morning. Why don't you come along with me, and we can talk in the plane? I'll tell you whatever I can. Maybe it'll be useful."

"That would be keen," said Danny. "What time shall we meet you?"

"Ten o'clock. But hold on. I'm afraid you

can't all come. I'm sorry, but you see, my plane's a little Piper Colt, a two-seater. I wish I could squeeze you all in, but there's only room for one passenger."

"I don't mind not going," Joe said. "I wouldn't be much good for this anyway. It's between Irene and Danny."

"Irene can go," Danny said gallantly. But his face was overcast as he spoke.

"No, that wouldn't be fair at all," said Irene. "We ought to choose between us somehow."

"Since you're so interested in science, why don't you do it scientifically?" Mr. Matthews suggested. "I know several scientists, and whenever they have an important choice to make they use a certain little device—"

"A computer?" Danny asked.

Mr. Matthews shook his head. Gravely, he dug into his pocket and brought out a half-dollar. "They toss a coin," he said.

"It doesn't seem very scientific," Irene said doubtfully.

"Will it help if I call it a 'circular, bipartite, limited-choice instrument'?" said Mr. Matthews. "Okay, that's what it is. Now, what do you say, heads or tails?"

"Heads," said Irene.

"Tails," Danny said.

Mr. Matthews flipped up the coin, caught it, and slapped it on the back of his other hand. "Tails it is," he announced.

"I'm sorry, Irene," said Danny, but he couldn't help the happy smile which spread over his face.

"Right. I've got to get going," Mr. Matthews said, picking up another cookie. "See you tomorrow at ten, at the airfield. You'll know my plane," he added, with a sorrowful sigh. "It'll be the one with patches all over it."

3
"A Peculiar Place to Park a Car"

Of course, Mr. Matthews had been joking. His plane was a bright red, trim little machine, as neat and shining as if it had just been washed. Danny climbed into the cockpit beside the pilot, and Mr. Matthews, after getting his clearance from the control tower, taxied out on one of the strips. Soon, they were soaring lightly over the end of the field and the town of Midston lay below them like a toy village, with the broad, silver platter of the reservoir lake to the south and the smooth, brown folds of the hills circling it on the north and east.

"In a little plane like this, you feel as though you're really flying," Danny said, peering out of the window beside him.

"Yes, I know what you mean," Mr. Matthews answered. "In one of those big commercial airplanes, you might as well be trav-

eling by train, for all the difference it makes. You're too high up, for one thing, and somehow you don't feel as if you have wings."

"Is this your own plane?" asked Danny.

Mr. Matthews nodded. "I came into a little money after I left the Air Force," he said, "and I bought a Piper Cub. Then, later, I turned it in for this one. It's my business, you know. I'm partners with a man named Abe Clark. We fly freight, and spray crops, and run a taxi service."

"And you work for the C.A.P. too," said Danny.

"Oh, that's volunteer work," Mr. Matthews said. "There are about twenty of us in the local squadron, some ex-Air Force pilots, some with private licenses. It's a kind of flying club. The squadron owns two planes, and there are five more owned by members. We are often called on to help various organizations, or to do special work for the state—like this fire patrol work I'm doing now. All we get out of this is that the state pays for our fuel."

They were now flying over a high hill called the Sugarloaf, and its bare, rocky summit gleamed like a bald head in the sunshine. The little plane seemed to go very slowly. It bounced a bit on the air currents, but it was only by watching the ground slide away beneath them that Danny had any sense of forward motion, and looking at the speedometer he was surprised to see that they were moving at seventy-five miles an hour.

"Do you always do fire patrolling?" he asked.

"Oh, no," said Mr. Matthews. "It has been an unusually dry year, and there's a good deal of danger from forest fires. So we've been asked to help out the wardens. You know, a few weeks ago there was a fire in the woods near Beckforth. I was the one who spotted that, and they were able to get it under control before it got too bad.''

He settled himself more comfortably in his seat and went on, ''Now, let's see. You wanted to know what makes a plane fly, is that it?''

''Well,'' said Danny, ''I sort of figured it must be the air itself which holds it up. But I don't understand how.''

''Not too difficult,'' Mr. Matthews said. He had a clipboard with a pad of paper attached to it, hanging from the instrument panel. He put it on his knee, took out his pencil, and quickly drew a rough sketch that looked like this:

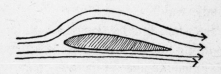

''That's the cross section of an airplane's wing,'' he explained. ''It's called the *airfoil*. Because of its shape and the fact that it is set at a slight angle, when the plane moves forward the air has farther to travel over the top of the wing than under its lower surface. That means that the air above is—well—sort of spread out, and thinner, while the air below is pushed together and is actually thicker. There's greater air pressure below the wing than above it. So the wing is pushed upward by the difference in pressure.

"If you are out riding your bike and you're coasting rapidly down a hill, you can test this by pointing the palm of your hand forward. Hold it rigid and flat and then angle the tips of your fingers upward a little. You'll feel the air push your hand up.

"Well, that's how a plane's wings operate. The motor pulls the plane forward swiftly and the air pressure lifts it up. Obviously, the faster you can go the more lift you'll have."

"I see," Danny said. "And a glider works the same way?"

"Yes, but gravity keeps a glider sliding downhill in the air," said Mr. Matthews. "The wings, pushing against the air, create the same lift and keep it flying. If it can hit a current of rising air, or a good wind, it can go faster and get more lift, and so rise still higher. Same thing with a kite."

Danny nodded. "I suppose a bird can soar the same way," he remarked.

"Well—yes," Mr. Matthews said slowly. "It's pretty much what happens when, say, a hawk rises on an air current. But a person, even one with wings attached to his arms, couldn't do the same thing. A bird has hollow bones, and powerful chest and wing muscles designed to give it the power to fly. We have to get that power from engines."

He pointed through the windshield at the propeller. "That's what pulls us ahead," he said. "If it were to stop, gravity would pull us down. Then, of course, the plane would act like a glider."

"I understand," said Danny.

"It helps if you think of air as a kind of fluid, like water almost," Mr. Matthews went on. "So when you stall, the wing acts as a spoiler and creates all kinds of burbles—"

"Huh? Burbles?"

"Mm. The air fuddles over the top of the wing and spills over and bubbles behind it—"

He broke off short, while Danny was still muttering, "Fuddles? Burbles?"

"What on earth is that?" Mr. Matthews said.

"Where?"

"Down there, in that field."

The airplane had swung round over Sugarloaf and the Midston Hills while they had been talking about flying, and Mr. Matthews had turned west. They were now above the rich farmland and thick woods that lay between Midston and the neighboring town of Derby. Just below them lay a wide stretch of pasture, flat and brown, with a pale gray ribbon of road running along beside it. And in the center of the pasture was a strange, gleaming, boxlike object surrounded by a jumble of black and white and brown forms.

Mr. Matthews tilted the plane and circled above the pasture.

"Cows—?" he said. "But what's that other thing?"

Danny craned his neck. "It's a car," he said. "A big, shiny car. A convertible. And there are cows all around it."

"What a peculiar place to park a car," said Mr. Matthews. "Look, you can see his tire marks, pale on the dry grass. He drove right in from the road. Why?"

"There's a man in the car," Danny said, staring down as they circled again. "He's standing on the seat. Look, he's waving at us. He's motioning us to come down."

"He must be crazy," Mr. Matthews said.

"But he must be in some kind of trouble," said Danny. "He's waving like anything." He pulled Mr. Matthews' sleeve. "You could land down there. It hasn't rained in so long the ground must be as hard as the airfield strip."

"Land? Down there?" Mr. Matthews frowned. "You're out of your mind."

"You mean there isn't enough room?"

"Sure, there's enough room. That field must be five hundred yards long and there aren't any trees. Just low stone walls. And it's all perfectly level."

"Oh. I see. You mean you aren't good enough to land in a field," Danny said, slyly.

"Mf! Grf!" Mr. Matthews spluttered. "Good enough? I can land this thing on a deck of playing cards. I can land it on a fifty cent piece. I can land it on a daisy without bending the petals. It's just that— I just don't— Oh, bother! Buckle your seat belt."

With that, he swung the airplane around in a graceful curve, banked so that the ground seemed to swing up, on one side of it, and then slid smoothly down to the pasture. The field skimmed past. The wheels touched, they bounced once or twice and rolled to a standstill.

"Gosh, that was beautiful, Mr. Matthews," Danny said enthusiastically.

"Oh, I don't know. Pretty terrible landing, I thought," said Mr. Matthews glumly, opening the door on his side of the cockpit.

They scrambled out of the plane. The cows had scattered when they came swooping in. They walked toward the automobile.

It was a Rolls Royce. It was immensely long, and its dark blue sides were as bright as mirrors. Its fittings were polished like silver, and its seats were covered with rich, heavy leather. Danny gave a long, low whistle.

The man who had been standing on the seat now hopped out of the car and strode toward them briskly.

"Good thing you came down when I waved," he barked.

"Are you in trouble?" asked Mr. Matthews.

"That's right. Need some help."

"What's wrong?"

"Lost my way," said the stranger. "Which way is it to Midston University?"

4
The Short-Cut Expert

Danny and Mr. Matthews stared at the man in speechless astonishment. He was rather short, with a wide mouth and large eyes, and a head that seemed too big for his body so that there was something vaguely froglike about him. There was, however, a suggestion of great energy, as well, which was not at all froglike; his manner was crisp and sharp as if he expected people to jump when he called them.

"Well?" he demanded, clasping his hands behind his back. "Speak up. Or don't you know? If not, say so."

Mr. Matthews gurgled feebly once or twice. Then he said, "Do you mean to say you wanted me to come down and land here just so that you could ask me the way to Midston?"

"Certainly. Why not?"

"Why not? Bring my plane down and make

a landing in a field full of cows just to answer a question you could have asked of the nearest passer-by—?''

"What's wrong with this field?" said the stranger. "Perfectly good field. And you *were* the nearest passer-by. Of course, you got rid of the cows for me, too. Had trouble with them. Couldn't drive clear of them. Hate cows. Grateful for that."

He pulled a wallet out of his pocket, flipped it open, and took out a bill. Danny's eyes opened wide. It was a hundred-dollar bill.

"Take this," the man said to Mr. Matthews. "Pay for your gas."

For a moment, it looked as though Mr. Matthews' head was about to burst from the pressure of his blood vessels. He turned absolutely purple, and his mouth opened and shut soundlessly. Then he regained control of himself and beckoned to Danny with one finger.

"Come on," he said. "Let's get out of here before I add murder to my many other crimes."

Danny was fascinated by someone who would park a Rolls Royce in a field, and could pull hundred-dollar bills out of his pocket. "Oh, please wait a minute, Mr. Matthews," he begged. "I'm sure this man didn't mean to insult you."

The stranger put his money away and snapped

his fingers. "My fault," he said. "Often act without thinking. Should have known you were a gentleman and wouldn't take money. Stupid of me. Sorry. Be friends." He thrust out one hand. "Accept apology. Can't say more, can I?"

Mr. Matthews hesitated. Then he shrugged. "Oh, well, as long as I'm here I may as well stay," he said. He took the other's hand and shook it. "But you must admit it was a crazy thing to do."

"Absolutely," said the strange. "Admit anything you like. Always have been crazy. Act on impulse. That's how I made my money. My name's Pippit—Glenway Pippit. What's yours?"

"Charles Matthews. And this is my friend, Danny Dunn."

"Very good." Mr. Pippit shook hands with Danny. "Glad to know you."

"How did you ever get into this field, sir?" Danny asked.

Mr. Pippit snorted. "Drove in, of course. Wanted to get to Midston University before noon. Saw what looked like a tower in the distance and decided to take a short cut. Always take short cuts. Can't resist 'em."

"This one hasn't done you any good," Danny said. "You've got to drive back up to the main road, then go east two miles, then take the first crossroad—that's Windmill Lane—then—''

"Stop!" cried Mr. Pippit. "Never will remember all that. Tell you what. Fly me to Midston. Pay you anything you like."

"What?" Mr. Matthews exclaimed.

"All right, no pay if that's how you want it," said Mr. Pippit.

"But—that's ridiculous. What would you do with your car?"

"Leave it. Buy another."

Mr. Matthews began to laugh. Danny said hastily, "You could give it to me. I mean, if you're just going to leave it here. I'd love to have a Rolls Royce convertible. I could keep it until I was old enough to drive."

"Hold on, Dan." Mr. Matthews wiped the tears of merriment from his eys, patting Danny's arm. "Mr. Pippit wouldn't have to throw the car away. He could always send a garageman after it. But it's impossible anyway. There isn't room in the airplane for the three of us, and I'm certainly not going to leave you here to walk home. No, a much simpler way is for us to finish our tour and then, when we land at the airfield, arrange for someone to drive out and guide Mr. Pippit to the university."

Mr. Pippit thrust out his chin aggressively. "What? Sit here for an hour or more? Can't be done. Got to meet the president of Midston at noon."

Danny had been eyeing the Rolls lovingly. "I could do it," he said.

"Do what? Wait here?" said Mr. Pippit.

"No, guide you to the college."

"Fine," Mr. Pippit snapped. "Jump in."

"Now, wait a minute," Mr. Matthews began.

"It's the best solution," Danny said. "I know the roads. And it really doesn't matter whether I go back with you or not. And—well—I've never driven in a car like this."

"Okay," said Mr. Matthews. "I can understand that. Maybe it wouldn't be such a bad idea. Go ahead, then. And if there's anything else you want to know about flying, telephone me."

"Thanks for everything, Mr. Matthews," Danny said. "Oh, boy! I feel the way Joe does when there are two desserts for dinner. First a plane ride, then a Rolls Royce."

He got into the car and Mr. Pippit jumped in and started the motor. As they drove out of the field, Mr. Matthews' engine roared and he taxied to the end of the pasture, turned his plane and took off. There was plenty of room and he soared up lightly, waggled his wings in farewell, and flew off.

For all his strange and peppery behavior, Mr. Pippit was a good driver and Danny enjoyed himself immensely. The day was mild and the wind refreshing; the car made almost no sound and went as smoothly as if, like the airplane, it wasn't touching the ground. Mr. Pippit had a way of firing off questions like bullets, and in the short time it took them to reach the edge of Midston he knew all about Danny's friends, his school, his friendship with Professor Bullfinch, and his interest in science.

"Want to be a scientist? Very good. Very good indeed," he said, lighting a cigar. "Rocketry. There's a good field. Interested in it myself. Got two plants turning out rocket engines."

"Oh, rocket engineering's all right," Danny said, "but I'm thinking of doing theoretical research."

"Rocketry," said Mr. Pippit firmly. "Only thing for a young man. Come and see me when you're a rocket expert."

"I'm more interested in the properties of matter," Danny said.

"Don't argue. Can't stand argument. Do whatever you want to. I need engineers in my business. They're more practical."

Danny began to feel his quick temper rising. "Professor Bullfinch says that applied science wouldn't get very far without theoretical science behind it," he said.

"Maybe so. Do I turn here?"

"Yes," said Danny, as they drew into the parking lot near the cluster of main buildings of the university.

As they got out of the car, Mr. Pippit said, "Know the quickest way to the president's office?"

"I know where it is," Danny replied. "I don't know if my way of getting there is the quickest way. It's a kind of short-cut I took once when I had to meet Professor Bullfinch—"

"A short cut? Fine!" Mr. Pippit tossed away his cigar and rubbed his hands together. "Show me."

Danny led the way to a side door. The offices of the university were part of a new wing which had been built on to the original College of Arts and Sciences, and Danny often followed the maze of corridors and hallways through the old building in order to visit scientists he knew, whose offices were in the opposite wing. But today, his mind was still running on his argument with Mr. Pippit, and he kept wondering how he could open the subject again without seeming to be impudent, and how he could convince the other that theoretical science was as important and valuable as engineering. The result was that he took the wrong stairway and suddenly realized that he was lost.

"What's the trouble?" asked Mr. Pippit, as Danny stopped.

"Why I—I'm not—" Danny stammered.

"Know where you're going?"

"Yes," Danny said desperately. Without stopping to think, he pulled open the nearest door. A stair led downward. He started down it with Mr. Pippit at his heels.

They emerged in a long, low-ceilinged basement room. It was lighted by a single dim bulb. Crates were piled along one wall, and at the far end was an open door. Danny realized that he ought to go back up the stairway, or at least confess that he didn't know where he was. But in his own way, he was every bit as headstrong as Mr. Pippit, and he didn't want to admit to this man who had no use for theoretical scientists that he was lost. So he plunged on, through the open door into another basement room as dim and dusty as the first.

Another door opened before them, on the right. This led through a long, cement corridor and finally into an echoing room full of machinery. Danny looked around in the hope of finding someone who could tell him how to get up to the daylight again, but there wasn't a soul in sight. Only the gleaming machines, which whirred and pounded and hummed to themselves.

"Doesn't look like the president's office," growled Mr. Pippit.

"We—have to go this way," Danny said. He went forward between the dark metal shapes, squeezing past their oily bulks, then along an iron catwalk which clattered underfoot. He came to a row of thick pipes covered with dirty asbestos wrappings, and climbed around them. Behind him, Mr. Pippit panted and grumbled, tripping now and then and bumping into things. Another room; this one full of cobwebby boxes, cleaning equipment, pails, and cardboard cartons. Then a spiral iron staircase appeared.

Danny began to climb. Mr. Pippit slipped on the greasy bottom step and said, "Drat, drat, DRAT!"

"It's only a little way farther," Danny said, by now past caring what happened.

"Double drat!" Mr. Pippit snarled.

The stair ended at a landing with a heavy, gray metal door. Danny pulled it open. He was standing in a corridor he recognized. There were the glass doors marked *Admissions Of-*

fice, and a short distance beyond them, a neat little sign projecting from the wall which said, *Office of the President.* Danny uttered a long sigh of relief.

"Here we are," he said, in the most casual tone he could manage.

He turned to Mr. Pippit. He gasped, and a chill breeze seemed to blow gently across his spine, freezing his cheerfulness.

Mr. Pippit was a wreck. His handsome gray suit was streaked with dust and splotched with oil. His hands were black with dirt and there was a smudge of grease across his face where he had wiped away the perspiration. His hair stuck up in untidy wisps that made his round head look even larger.

But it was obvious he did not know what he looked like. He didn't even notice Danny's startled look. Glancing about, he saw the sign and snapped his fingers.

"Good!" he said. "Hard work, but worth it. A great short cut."

He put out his hand and Danny shook it automatically.

"Many thanks," said Mr. Pippit. "See you again. Remember, come visit me when you know something about rockets."

Without another word, he marched across the hall and entered the president's office.

Sooner or later, Danny knew, there was going to come a roar from that office, either when Mr. Pippit met the president, or more likely, when the president's secretary stared at him in amazement. Before that happened, Danny decided, it would be best if he were far, far away. He began walking rapidly toward the main hallway, but before he had left the building he was running as fast as he could.

5
The Laser

As soon as he had wolfed down his lunch, Danny ran next door to the Millers' house. Mrs. Miller, a small, plump woman with bright and happy blue eyes, answered his knock.

"Hullo, Dan," she said. "Irene's been expecting you. Go right up."

Irene's room looked as though two people with different tastes shared it. It was a rather long room with large windows, and one half of it was very feminine, with a pleasant maple dresser, a four-poster bed covered with a patchwork comforter, a pair of frilly armchairs, and a large framed reproduction of a Degas pastel drawing of ballet dancers. The other half contained two big bookcases crammed with books, an amateur radio receiver and broadcasting set, and a long workbench strewn with such odds and ends as an electromagnet, a dismantled phonograph turntable, and a model platetarium. It was much neater than Danny's room, however, and much easier to be comfortable in.

Irene looked up from a book. "Hi," she said. "What time is it—brillig?"

"Yep," Danny said, dropping into the other chair. "And the slithy toves are gyring and gimbling in the wabe. Still reading *Alice in Wonderland?*"

"I never seem to get tired of it. How did things go with Mr. Matthews?"

"Up in the air," Danny grinned.

"What? You mean nothing was settled?"

"No, I just couldn't resist the joke. Everything was fine, except for Mr. Pippit." And he told her of his adventures.

"Oh, dear. And so you ran off before he could discover how dirty he was?" Irene gave a shriek of laughter, clapping her hands to her cheeks. "I know I shouldn't laugh at the poor man, but I can't help thinking of his face when he found out how he looked."

"Yes, that was what I was thinking of," said Danny, "only it wouldn't have been so funny for me. Anyway, I found out from Mr.

41

Matthews what holds a plane up. It's a difference in air pressure above and below the wing, and it depends on the speed with which the plane moves forward." He explained in detail, sketching the same airfoil pattern for Irene that the pilot had drawn for him.

"I see." Irene rested her chin on her fist. "Now the question is, how do we demonstrate this for the science fair?"

They sat in deep thought for a few minutes, and Danny said, "Mr. Matthews kept saying we ought to think of air as a kind of fluid. If we could take a model plane, for instance, and somehow put it in a tank of water—"

"It would get awfully soggy," said Irene. "Why couldn't we just *fly* a plane model?"

"You wouldn't see how the air lifts it, then." Danny stared at the drawing he had made. "What we need is a wing—an airfoil. And then some way of showing the air moving at it, and lifting it—I know!" He clapped his hands. "A wind tunnel! We'll make a wind tunnel."

"You mean, like the kind they use in aeronautical laboratories?"

"Something like that." Danny seized a pencil and began to make a sketch of the plan as he spoke. "A long box, open at each end, with a window in one side so you can look in. There are some long panes of glass in our basement, and we could cover the window opening with one of them. Inside, we put a model of an airplane wing, mounted on a wire so that it will move easily, up or down. We put an electric fan at one end of the box, and when we turn it on the air makes the wing rise.''

"I see. Good. We ought to make the box, or tunnel, out of sheet metal, folded into shape. It will be sturdier that way." Irene hummed to herself for a moment, studying his sketch. "You know what we need? Something to make the air visible."

"Huh? How?"

"I mean people ought to see how the air actually flows over and under the wing. We could do it with smoke. If we could make a thick smoke and let it blow through the electric fan, people could see the way the air currents move."

"A dandy idea," said Danny. "What makes smoke—without setting fire to the whole thing?"

"Burning kerosene-soaked rags in a tin can?"

"Woof! Smelly."

"What about burning sulphur? That would give a nice yellow smoke."

"Might be poisonous, too. Tell you what:

let's go over to my house and ask Professor Bullfinch. Maybe he'll have a suggestion."

Irene hesitated. "Gee, I don't know, Dan. We really ought to do all the rest of the research ourselves. It doesn't seem right somehow, to keep asking grownups for information."

Danny lay back in his chair. "No, I don't agree," he said, crossing his ankles. "Once I was watching the Professor prepare a problem to be fed into a computer. I said to him, 'Golly, Professor Bullfinch, you must know *every-thing*!' He laughed. He said, 'I know a little bit about several things, but nobody can know everything. I don't even think it would be much fun to know everything. But there are two important things everyone should know. They are: where to go for information, and what to do with the information when you get it.'

"We could look in some chemistry books and try a lot of experiments, but that would take a lot more time than asking the Professor would. If he makes a couple of suggestions, we can try them out. Scientists use computers for the same reason—to save time. Going to people isn't any worse than going to the books people write, or the computers they invent."

"All right, you've convinced me." Irene got to her feet. "Let's go. Stop making yourself so comfortable. Now who's wasting time?"

"It's just that this chair is so nice," Danny said. Nevertheless, he got up.

"Why, you've got an armchair just like it in your room," Irene said.

"I know. But whenever I want to sit in it, I have to take all the books off it, and that's too much trouble."

Professor Bullfinch had a private laboratory built on to the back of his house and connected with it by a short hallway. The laboratory was divided into two rooms, a small one full of books and notebooks which served as a study, and a larger one in which were stone-topped lab benches and a variety of equipment used for research and experiment. When the two young people entered the laboratory by the back door, Professor Bullfinch was fussing over a curious-looking apparatus.

Professor Bullfinch did not look in the slightest like the scientists one sees in television shows: he was neither young and crisp, nor bearded and dignified. He did not wear a white smock, but a tweed jacket and brown slacks. He was rather tubby, with a round, merry face and a bald head, and behind his glasses twinkled a pair of kindly eyes that somehow missed nothing that went on around him. He straightened up from the machine he had been working on, dusted his palms together, and smiled.

"Hello, Dan," he said. "How are you, Irene? Looking for me, were you? Or just passing through?"

"We were looking for you, Professor, for some information," said Irene.

Danny was already bending over the workbench, examining the Professor's apparatus. "Gosh, what's this?" he said. "I can't figure it out. Some kind of slide projector?"

There was a square black box, with a second, larger box near it, the two connected by a heavy cable. The smaller box had a tube projecting from one end of it, with what appeared to be a lens on it.

"It does look a bit like a projector," the Professor admitted. "Actually, it's a laser."

"A lazer?" Danny blinked. "Something to make people lazy? Or something to make lazy people wake up?"

"No, no. The word *laser* stands for 'light amplification by stimulated emission of radiation.' Some scientists call it the 'death ray.'"

"A death ray?" Irene's eyes opened wide. "Is it really?"

"Oh, dear, no. It's just a sort of joke we have." He lifted the black box and they could see that it was really only a cover for what looked like a red glass rod, around which four long, odd-looking lamps were arranged. "Here,

46

in the center, is an artificial crystal of calcium fluoride,'' he explained. ''It's one of the largest ever made in the laboratory. Around it I have four mercury vapor lamps which make an extremely bright light. The inside of the case is highly polished, to increase the light. The other box contains my own invention, a new kind of high-voltage power source. Power is carried to the lamps by this cable.

''The device was developed from an instrument invented by Professor Townes of Columbia University in 1954, which amplified microwaves. Another name for it is 'optical maser'—a name many scientists prefer. It is rather difficult to explain simply, but what happens is that the lights, flashing on around the crystal, cause the electrons in the atoms in it to bounce around like mad. Eventually, when they are 'pumped up,' as you might say, to the proper state, a flash of light escapes through a little opening in the silver which coats the end of the crystal. It's something like water under pressure coming out of a hose. The interesting thing about this beam of light is that it is parallel—that is, it is concentrated so that the same amount that starts from the crystal arrives at the end of the beam. Do you see? Now, by means of a rather complicated lens system which I developed, this light, which is red, is still more concentrated and produces intense heat. Up to now, optical masers have only been operated in short bursts, but by means of a special cooling system I can operate this one continuously. This is a new development in the field, and I must admit I am feeling rather proud of myself." And Professor Bullfinch grinned modestly, and rubbed his bald head with one hand.

Danny had been pondering the Professor's words, and now he said, "Well, golly! If it produces heat—why, it's a sort of heat ray, isn't it?"

"Yes, actually it is," said the Professor. "I have just finished testing it because I am expecting some important visitors and I want to demonstrate how it works. Now, what was it you wanted to find out from me? I hope it isn't anything complicated, because I'm afraid I really haven't much time now."

"We don't know how complicated it is," said Irene. "We want to make a thick white smoke—but not too thick."

"Thick, but not too thick." Professor Bullfinch looked puzzled. "You mean a smoke screen?"

"Not exactly. We're going to make a wind tunnel to demonstrate how a plane flies,"

Danny said. "We want to show, by means of smoke, the movement of the air currents."

"I see. Well, you might try placing an open beaker full of ammonia next to another open beaker full of hydrochloric acid. The fumes from the two will blend to form a fairly good white smoke. If you paint the inside walls of your wind tunnel red, or blue, the smoke will show up nicely. Naturally, you'd better leave both ends of the tunnel open, and be sure no one is standing in the path of that smoke."

"It sounds great," Danny said. "Let's try it right now. You must have hydrochloric acid in the laboratory, Professor. I'll go get some ammonia from Mom, in the kitchen."

"Well, I'm not sure I have enough time for—" Professor Bullfinch began.

But Danny was already at the door, his head full of nothing but the idea and how it might work. He pulled the door open and charged recklessly through.

There were two men standing in the hallway, and one of them was just reaching out his hand for the knob of the laboratory door.

"Look out!" Irene screamed, but she was too late.

Danny crashed headlong into them, and all three went down in a heap. For a moment, all that could be seen were arms and legs waving in the air. Then Danny pulled himself free and scrambled to his hands and knees. At the same time, one of the men sat up straight, red-faced and glowering.

"You again?" he snapped.

It was Mr. Pippit.

6
The Professor
Loses His Temper

For a moment, Danny was tempted to escape. Then, coming to his senses, he began to babble his apologies. Mr. Pippit cut him short.

"Never mind that. Help Mr. Richards up. He's lying on my leg."

Mr. Richards, the president of Midston University, was tall and fat, and Danny had knocked all the wind out of him. Puffing and panting, he was trying to sit up. Danny took his arm, and an instant later Professor Bullfinch was at his side. Between them, they helped him rise. Mr. Pippit jumped up spryly and began dusting off his trousers.

"Expected a hearty greeting," he crackled. "But didn't expect to be swept off my feet."

"Are you all right, Mr. Richards?" Professor Bullfinch asked anxiously.

"Yes, yes, quite all right. An accident, I'm sure," said the president. He looked ruefully at Danny. "Dear me, Daniel, you're as lively and impulsive as ever, I see."

"I'm awfully sorry, Mr. Richards," Danny stammered.

"I'm sure you are. I'm not concerned for myself, but for our distinguished visitor."

"Distinguished visitor my foot," said Mr. Pippit. "Don't care for flattery. Never have. This boy has already ruined one suit for me. Led me on a wild chase through the cellars. Now he bowls us over like tenpins. What's he doing here? Why?"

Professor Bullfinch raised his eyebrows. "You've met Danny already?"

"Showed me the way to Midston. Took a short cut to Richards' office. Almost never came to the surface again. Didn't expect to find him at an important conference like this."

"Danny is here because he lives in this house, Mr. Pippit," said the Professor. "I'm sure that whatever happened this morning, he meant no harm."

"You said yourself that you can't resist short cuts, Mr. Pippit," said Danny. "That's how you got into that field, with all those—"

"Never mind that," Mr. Pippit broke in, getting a little pink. "Admit it was partly my own fault. Can't say more. Forget the whole thing. Get to business."

Professor Bullfinch ushered them into the laboratory. Mr. Richards said, "Mr. Pippit is very anxious to see the laser, Professor. I have been able to explain it only very sketchily, naturally."

"I have it all ready," said Professor Bullfinch. "If you will step this way, I'll be glad to demonstrate its action."

"Good," said Mr. Pippit. "But chase the kids out. Don't want them breathing down my neck."

The Professor said mildly, "These two young people are very interested in science. They know how the laser works in theory, and I'm sure they'd like to see the demonstration. They are both very well behaved and I know they won't be in the way."

"Don't care about behavior. That boy carries disaster around with him. If he's here, the thing's liable to explode."

"That's impossible. The laser cannot explode," said the Professor, stiffly.

It was clear to Danny, who knew him well, that the Professor was beginning to be a little annoyed with Mr. Pippit's high-handed manner.

"Professor Bullfinch, I've made enough trouble already," the boy said, quickly. "I don't mind going. Maybe Mr. Pippit is right. Come on, Irene."

He caught her by the hand and dragged her to the back door. As soon as they were outside, he whisked her around the angle of the building.

"Why'd you do that?" she demanded. "The Professor would have insisted, and we could have stayed. I'd like to see how the laser operates."

"You will," said Danny. "But listen. That Pippit man is rich and important, and I'll bet he's here because they want him to give some money to the university. Maybe it has something to do with the Professor's research. If they got into a fight because of me, I'd—I just wouldn't know what to do. Nobody would say anything, but they would all know it was my fault. This way, we can watch the demonstration anyway and nobody will know about it. We'll go in through the window of the other room where the Professor keeps his books. If we keep quiet, we can see everything from the doorway."

As silently as an Indian, Danny pushed up the window and wriggled over the sill. Irene followed him. He closed the window softly so that not even a breeze would betray them. They tiptoed to the door which was open and peered round the corner.

The Professor had covered his machine again, and had set up in front of it a wooden rack holding a row of framed white squares, one behind the other and about a foot apart. Mr. Pippit, with his hands in his pockets, stood with his head on one side and his eyes half closed. Mr. Richards kept nodding and smiling, but he was watching Mr. Pippit instead of Professor Bullfinch or the machine.

". . . so that in effect," the Professor was saying, "we will have a tight beam of concentrated red light, traveling at the speed of light." He pointed to the white squares. "When I throw the power on, you will be able to see the nature of the beam because it will burn perfectly round holes of the same diameter as the beam through each of these plastic squares. There will be no spreading as there would be in a beam of reflected light, from a flashlight, say."

"Won't the squares go up in flames?" asked Mr. Pippit.

"No. They have been treated so that the beam will simply melt them away where it touches."

The Professor glanced at the dial on his power supply. Then he thumbed a switch. There was a sharp *pop!* Dan and Irene saw a flash leap from the tube of the laser. It lasted for a fraction of a second. The Professor indicated the plastic squares.

"You may examine them for yourself, Mr. Pippit," he said.

Mr. Pippit took two or three of the squares out of the long rack that held them. Through

the center of each was punched a neat hole about the diameter of a pencil.

"Hmm. Very interesting," he said.

"Now," the Professor continued, "I will operate the laser continuously for a few seconds, instead of in one short burst."

He removed the plastic squares. On a stone-topped lab bench at the other end of the room he put a block of wood painted white.

"This will demonstrate the fact that the beam also transmits the energy involved, in the form of heat," he said.

He aimed the laser at the block, squinted along it, and snapped the switch. This time, the machine hissed like a snake. The young people, from their hiding place, could clearly see a pale reddish rod of light that sprang from the laser and struck the block of wood. A smell of burning filled the air and a plume of smoke

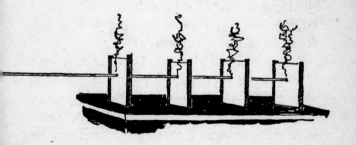

went up from the wood. The Professor shut off the laser. There was a charred black hole in the center of the white block.

Professor Bullfinch smiled and took out his old briar pipe. He began to fill it. "Any questions?" he asked, as if he were addressing a classroom.

"A remarkable device, my dear Bullfinch," said Mr. Richards. "Very impressive indeed. Don't you agree, Mr. Pippit?"

"Quite a trick," grunted Mr. Pippit. "What good is it?"

"Eh?" The Professor stopped in the act of lighting his pipe. "What good? Well, I—I'm afraid we haven't actually decided that yet. I'm sure there will be many uses for the laser. Dr. Schawlow, one of those who developed the optical maser, suggests that it may be used to synthesize wave lengths that cannot be produced directly—"

"Don't understand all that fancy stuff," said Mr. Pippit. "Could it be used in war?"

"In war?" The Professor's voice grew frosty. "I'm afraid I don't understand."

"Very simple. It's a kind of heat ray, isn't it? Could you set fire to an enemy missile with it?"

The Professor's normally jolly face darkened. He was silent for a moment, and then he said, "Mr. Pippit, science is concerned with making man's life better, not ending it. The aim of research is to learn—to learn more about ourselves, about matter, about man's place in the universe. The laser is a valuable and interesting tool in learning more about the properties of light. Engineers working with it will undoubtedly develop it further and apply it in a variety of useful ways. But I hope with all my heart they never turn it into a weapon."

"A good sentiment," said Mr. Pippit. He tightened his lips, thrusting his big head forward at the Professor, his hands clasped firmly behind his back. "However, I'm a practical man. Not interested in theories. Planning to give a million dollars to Midston for a Research Center. Don't want 'em researching hairbrained schemes or throwing the money away on highbrow nonsense."

"The laser is not a hair-browed scheme," said the Professor. He was, by now, so angry that he stumbled over his words. "I mean it is *not* highbrained." He caught himself and took a deep breath. Then he said more calmly, "I'm afraid we don't see eye to eye on the question of scientific research, Mr. Pippit."

Mr. Pippit glanced at his watch. "No. Want to talk to you again, Professor. Got to go, now. Must send a couple of telegrams, and want to see the work of some of your other men. We'll discuss this further in a few days. Pleasure to meet you. Coming, Richards?"

"I—I'll be with you in a moment, Mr. Pippit," Mr. Richards said, in a worried voice. "I—um—must just discuss something in private with the Professor. It will only take a minute—"

"I'll wait for you in the car. Sixty seconds precisely."

Mr. Pippit nodded his head at the Professor, and left the room.

Mr. Richards sighed. "My dear Bullfinch," he said, "I want you to know that I quite understand your position. But for heaven's sake, be cautious. A million dollars! That's an enormous amount of money. For the sake of the university, try to pocket your pride."

"Pride?" said the Professor. "It has nothing to do with pride. That man is a monster!"

"Perhaps he is. But the Research Center is more important than your feeling about science. We must fight fire with fire. We must be moderate. Please try to think of some practical uses for the laser. I'm sure that will satisfy Mr. Pippit."

Mr. Richards hurried out. The Professor sank into a chair. Then he snorted, and lit his pipe.

"Fight fire with fire indeed!" he said aloud. "Shame on you, Bullfinch. That's the first time you've lost your temper in ten years."

He sighed, tossed away the match, and puffed out a huge cloud of smoke to relieve his feelings.

7
Snitcher Asks for Help

Danny gave a last turn of the screw driver to the last of the bolts which held a sheet of metal to a wooden framework, and stepped back.

"There," he said. "Done. And not a bad job, if I say so myself."

Since Sunday afternoon, he and Irene—with occasional help from Joe—had worked on the wind tunnel, using what time they could after school, sandwiched in between homework and other attractions. Now, on Wednesday, they had finished the job. The tunnel was about four feet long and a foot square, and open at both ends. Three sides were solid, but the fourth contained a long window made of thick, transparent plastic. They had bought this from a hardware store since it was lighter and less fragile than glass. The top of the tunnel was hinged and fastened with a hook, so that they could reach the inside easily.

"The only thing it needs now," said Irene, "is a coat of paint on the outside to make it look trim. Then we can start on the model airplane wing."

"We'll have to figure out how to support it so that it will move easily, lift up and drop, but still won't blow away," said Danny. "I'll work on that part if you'll make the wing. You're better than I am on delicate jobs."

"Okay," Irene agreed. She began to stir the can of blue paint with which they had already painted the inside of the tunnel.

Danny took up a brush and cocked an eye at Joe, who was lounging on a crate in a corner of the basement workshop, eating an apple.

"You don't have to look at me like that," Joe protested. "I've already worked hard on this thing. I put in two bolts and painted one whole panel of the inside."

"Come on, Joe, don't be so lazy," Irene coaxed.

"I'm not lazy," he said. "Work makes me hungry, and then the smell of paint spoils my appetite. It's a vicious circle."

Nevertheless, he pitched away the core of

his apple and took the brush. "The things I do for my friends," he grumbled. "I could be writing a famous poem that would go down through the ages, instead of slaving away at this gruesome job."

Danny began collecting the tools. "I'm worried about Professor Bullfinch," he said, moodily.

"Still no word from Mr. Pippit?" Irene asked.

"No. He's still here in town, but he hasn't met with the Professor again. I heard the Professor talking to Mr. Richards on the phone this afternoon, and he said he's 'thinking about the matter.' I wish we could help him."

"Well, just get that wish out of your head," Joe said, swabbing away with his paint brush. They had described the laser to him, and told him about the disagreement between Professor Bullfinch and Mr. Pippit. "Every time you decide to help somebody, I begin looking for a table to crawl under."

"You sound like Mr. Pippit," Danny said.

"Maybe I am Mr. Pippit," said Joe. "Wouldn't that be nice? I'd have my butler do this paint job, while I took a little spin in the country in my Rolls Royce."

"It shouldn't be that difficult to think of practical uses for the laser," Irene put in. "For instance, I should think you could use it as a kind of welding machine.''

"Sure, but that isn't so practical," said Danny. "It wouldn't do anything a regular welding machine couldn't do. Oh, maybe you could weld something after it had been sealed up inside a glass tube. But that isn't what Mr. Pippit is after. He wants an idea he can make lots of money with.''

"How about a long-range cigarette lighter?" Joe suggested.

"Huh? How would that work?''

"Easy. Say there are two men working in a big room. The first man takes out a cigarette and hollers over to the other, 'Got a light?' The second man takes out his laser and shoots a beam across the room—''

"And if he misses the cigarette he sets fire to the first man's head," said Danny. "I don't think that's what Mr. Pippit has in mind.''

"You're hard to satisfy," said Joe. "I give you a perfectly good idea and you turn it down. Okay, how about using it to punch holes in something at long distance?''

"Punch holes in what, for instance?" asked Danny.

"How should I know? I just make theory. It's up to you to figure out the details," Joe grinned.

The basement door opened, and Mrs. Dunn called down the stair, "Dan? Are you still down there?"

"Yes, Mom."

"One of your school friends is here to see you. Shall I send him down, or will you come up?"

"Send him down," said Danny.

"Who on earth—?" Irene began.

Down the stairs, making a clatter like a galloping horse, came Snitcher Philips.

He stood looking around him with a curious, half-sheepish, half-defiant expression. At last he said, "Hi."

"Hello," said Danny, without moving.

"I suppose you're pretty surprised to see me here," Eddie said.

"Well, yeah. Sort of."

Joe and Irene said nothing at all. Eddie had come to Danny's house, and that made it Danny's problem.

Eddie stuck his hands in his trouser pockets, and hunched his shoulders. "Well, the fact is," he said, "I need some help. We've never been exactly what you'd call friends, but you know a lot about science. More than I do. I want to make a display for the Science Fair, and I'm—I guess I'm sort of stuck. I want to make a model showing how two atoms of hydrogen combine with one atom of oxygen to make a molecule of water. But I can't find a diagram anywhere that shows how the oxygen atom looks.''

Danny stared at him. There was silence, for a while.

At last, shifting awkwardly from foot to foot, Eddie said, ''Oh, well, if you're gonna hold it against me that we had a few fights—''

''No,'' Danny said, hastily. ''Not at all. It's just that I'm kind of dazed. That's all. I didn't expect—well, sure I'll help you. You know how an atom of hydrogen looks?''

'' 'Course. That one's simple: one electron revolving around one proton in the nucleus.''

''Uh-huh. How are you going to make it?''

''I'll use a marble for the nucleus, or maybe a Ping-pong ball, and show the path of the electron with a wire circle.''

''Okay. Well, an atom of oxygen has eight protons and eight neutrons in the nucleus. And it has eight electrons shooting around it.''

''I see. And the electrons would circle the nucleus?''

''Sure. Nobody knows what the atom really looks like anyway, so your guess is as good as anybody's.''

Eddie nodded. ''Gee, thanks a lot. That's real swell of you.''

His gaze wandered to the wind tunnel. "You building something for the Fair?" he asked.

Irene shot Danny a warning glance. But Dan was feeling warm and friendly, and saw no need to be cautious. "Yes, that's going to be our display," he said. "You remember when we had that argument about what makes a plane fly?"

"Oh, that. I remember. What of it?"

"We did some research and found out what does hold a plane up in the air."

"I said it was the engine."

"Yes, but you were wrong. The engine helps, but a glider doesn't have an engine. Right? It's the shape of the wing. When the plane moves forward, the air rushing at the wing takes longer to pass over it than under it. This means the air pressure is less on top of

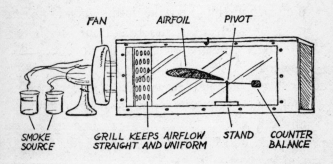

FAN   AIRFOIL   PIVOT

SMOKE SOURCE   GRILL KEEPS AIRFLOW STRAIGHT AND UNIFORM   STAND   COUNTER BALANCE

the wing than underneath. Come over here and I'll show you how this thing will work."

He and Eddie walked across the basement, and Danny explained the wind tunnel's operation.

"Say, that's neat," Eddie said, with admiration shining on his face. "Yes, sir, I gotta hand it to you. That's a real clever idea."

"Thanks," said Danny. "Of course, Irene is partly responsible for it. We're sharing it."

"Yeah. Well, I've got to go," Eddie said. "So long. And thanks a lot for the help."

He waved a hand at the other two, and climbed the stairs to the basement door.

When he had gone, Danny said, "Well, I guess I was wrong. Eddie's not such a bad sort of guy after all."

"Maybe you're right," Irene agreed. "But I hope our project didn't give him any unexpected ideas."

8
"It's Our
Wind Tunnel!"

Friday the thirteenth was the day of the unpleasant surprise.

When the Science period began, Miss Arnold said, "Class, I have an important announcement to make. You will remember that I asked you to bring your exhibits for the Science Fair to school as soon as you could. And I also said that I'd invite our principal, Mr. Standish, to visit us when the first exhibit arrived. Well, that day has come. I must say, it's come a good deal sooner than I expected and the boy who has his project ready deserves a good deal of credit."

A buzz went round the classroom, as people turned and stared at each other and whispered,

"Who is it?" "Do you know?" "No, do you?"

The classroom door opened for Mr. Standish and Mrs. Roth, who was the assistant principal. The class grew still, and Miss Arnold led the guests to the chairs which had been set out for them.

Before sitting down, Mr. Standish cleared his throat and said, "We are very pleased to be here, Miss Arnold. I knew your class would turn in some exciting material, and we're looking forward to seeing this first display. I want to remind the young people that science is more than just a school subject. It is a way of looking at life and trying to understand it. Now, I won't give a long speech today so you needn't start fidgeting around. I merely wish to offer my congratulations to the student who worked so hard to get this exhibit ready so quickly."

He beamed, and sat down. Miss Arnold said, "Very well, Eddie. You may go and get your project. George, you may help him carry it."

Eddie Philips, wearing a wide cat-grin, got up and left the room, with George Bessel following him.

"Whew!" Danny whispered to Joe, who sat in front of him. "He must have worked like a slave on that atomic model."

"Yes. But it wasn't too hard to make," Joe

71

returned. "Just a bunch of balls and some wire."

Irene, who sat next to Dan, said across the aisle, "Let's wait and see what it looks like. It may be more complicated than you think."

"We'll soon see," Danny said. "Here they come."

The two boys came back into the room. Between them, they carried a long, red box, open at both ends.

Danny began to get up, his mouth opening in protest. Joe pulled him down again.

"But it's—it's *our* wind tunnel!" Danny gulped.

"Shh!" said Joe. "It's a wind tunnel, all right, but not yours. Yours is blue. Anyway, you can't say anything in front of Mr. Standish. It'll just look as though you're jealous."

Irene was blushing with indignation, but she held herself in check. She leaned over to Danny and said softly, "Did you register our idea with Miss Arnold?"

He clapped a hand to his forehead. "Oh, golly, I forgot. I was going to do it on Monday, and all I could think of was getting the sheet of plastic from the hardware store."

"That's what I was afraid of," said Irene. "When Eddie saw our project, he must have decided it was better than his. Then he checked with Miss Arnold and found that it hadn't been registered with her, so he decided he'd get there first."

Danny groaned. "Well, there's no law that says he can't," he said gloomily. "It's my own fault for not having told Miss Arnold what we were working on."

Eddie and George were setting up the wind tunnel on a table facing an open window. It was a more elaborate construction than Danny's and Irene's, being made of plywood, trimly finished and painted, with one whole side neatly fitted with glass instead of plastic. The whole thing was bound with shining copper strips. Instead of a model wing, there was a small glider mounted on a wire stand inside. Eddie put a tin container in one end and set up an electric fan in front of it.

"How did he get it done so quickly? That's what I can't understand," said Joe. "He isn't that good at making things. And that one's much fancier than yours."

"I can guess," Danny replied, bitterly. "Eddie's father is a building contractor. I'll bet you he put a couple of his carpenters on the job and they built it for him in no time. I wonder what the tin can is for?"

Eddie stood before the class. For a moment,

his eyes met Danny's and then he blushed and glanced away.

"Well, now," he said, "this is a wind tunnel. It demonstrates how a plane flies. I am going to blow air through the box with this electric fan. I will light some oily rags in this tin can to make smoke so that you can see how the air moves around the wings of the glider and lifts it."

Danny snorted. "So that's it! That's the one thing I didn't tell him—how we were going to make the smoke. I guess he can get credit for *that*, anyway."

Mr. Standish, Mrs. Roth, and Miss Arnold stood up so that they could see better. The children in the back of the room moved down to desks nearer the front, doubling up with their friends. Irene was gnawing her handkerchief in anger, and Danny kept punching his fist into his palm and growling under his breath. Eddie carefully lighted a match and touched it to the oily rags. Dark, greasy smoke coiled up.

"You can see that the plane is just hanging loosely on its wire stand," Eddie said, tapping the glass panel with a pencil. "Now we'll start the fan, and you will see the plane rise."

Miss Arnold was beginning to look nervously at the ceiling, where the smoke was making a sooty circle. Before she could say anything, Eddie snapped on the electric fan.

Perhaps the fan was more powerful than Eddie had anticipated. Or perhaps the little wire stand had not been fastened securely in place. First, it blew straight out. Then, with a clatter, the model sailed right through the wind tunnel with the wire stand behind it, and vanished out of the open window.

"Hey!" yelled George. "Grab it!"

"Watch out for that tin can!" Danny cried, jumping to his feet.

The draft had fanned the rags into flame. At the same moment, Eddie made a grab for the model. He knocked over the fan and fell sprawling. The fan knocked over the tin can. A spout of flame shot through the wind tunnel.

Danny was already out of his seat and in the hall. A foam-type fire extinguisher hung on its bracket near the classroom door. Dan grabbed it and ran back into the room with it.

The whole thing had happened so rapidly that no one else had moved. But as Danny rushed back in, Mrs. Roth screamed. Mr. Standish whirled around to find the fire extinguisher and collided with Miss Arnold who had had the same idea. Danny darted around them, and pressed down the trigger of the extinguisher. In seconds, the fire was out.

Eddie got to his feet wiping his head and face, for he had been spattered by the foam. The rest of the class was babbling with excitement. Irene caught Danny's arm.

"Are you all right?" she asked.

"Quick thinking, young man," said Mr. Standish, coming up behind them. He patted Dan's shoulder. "Not a spark left. You ought to get a medal for that. But too bad about the demonstration."

Miss Arnold appeared. She had been inspecting the mess—the scorched box, the ruined electric fan, the pools and blobs of foam all over the table, floor, and window. She had had some of the children open the other windows to remove the smell of smoke.

She said, in the calm, chilly voice she used when she was particularly annoyed, "Eddie."

"Yes ma'am," he said. Big as he was, he seemed to shrink to the size of a first-grader.

"I want to ask you something. Did you test this apparatus before you brought it to class today?"

"Well—" Eddie looked at the ceiling, and around the classroom, and then at Mr. Standish. At last, with his eyes on the floor, he said, "No, ma'am."

Mr. Standish clucked. "Well, well," he said. "That's a different matter."

"Exactly," said Miss Arnold. "This was an accident that happened because of plain carelessness. If it hadn't been for Danny, the only one of us who was alert to the danger, the whole classroom might have gone up in smoke. It could all have been avoided if Eddie had tried out his wind tunnel first. Then he'd have found out what was wrong and corrected it."

She took a long breath. "Perhaps it's as much my fault as his. But I gave my students credit for being careful enough to test out their projects before showing them. Eddie, you can clean up this mess, now. I'm sorry you had to come down for nothing, Mr. Standish. We'll be much more careful in the future."

Joe said, in Danny's ear, "Poor old Snitch. He was in too much of a hurry. Even after he swiped the idea, he was afraid he might not get here first with it. What are you going to do now? Tell Miss Arnold about it?"

Danny shook his head. "No, I'm not going to do anything. He's had his punishment."

Irene smiled at him. "You're right," she said. "For a minute, I wanted to—oooh, just kill him. I could have bashed him with a chair. But now I feel sort of sorry for him."

Joe snickered. "His name should be changed from *Snitcher*."

"To what?" asked Danny.

"To *Mud*."

Irene laughed. But Danny suddenly frowned, intently.

"Mud," he repeated. "Hey, what an idea. *Mud!* That's the solution."

Joe blinked. "Huh? A solution of mud? What kind of a solution is that?"

Danny swung the fire extinguisher, which he had been holding all this time. He chuckled.

"The practical use for the laser," he said. "I'll tell you later. I've got to put this extinguisher back."

Joe gaped after him. "I don't get it," he said to Irene. "He baffles me. Is he thinking of using the laser to bake mud pies?"

"We'll talk about it after school," said Irene. "We'd better get back to our seats. Miss Arnold is beginning to get that look in her eye that means thunderstorms coming."

9
Irene Tries Glamor

On the way home from school they stopped at Joe's house, at his insistence, to pick up the notebook in which he wrote his poems. Joe wanted to be a writer when he grew up, and was well known in school for the poetry he composed.

"I want to have the notebook handy," he explained, stuffing it in his back pocket, "because maybe I'll think of some rhymes for laser. And don't say 'blazer' because I've got that," he added.

"Are you making a poem about it?" Danny asked.

"Uh-huh. Might come in handy. If Mr. Pippit decides to buy the thing, maybe he can use a good poem to celebrate it."

Irene said, "While we're on the subject,

Danny, tell us your idea for a practical use for the laser. Don't be so mysterious. What did you mean by a muddy solution?''

Danny tapped the side of his nose with a forefinger. ''One of my best ideas,'' he said. ''This is so good it scares me.''

''Hmm,'' muttered Joe. ''Should I start running now?''

''Take it easy. Now, look, you know Burton's Bog?''

''The big marshy place near Mr. Glenn's farm?'' said Irene. ''Of course. The place where they say a cow once sank in and vanished in the quicksand.''

''Yep. Well, there must be hundreds—thousands—of such places all over the country. They're no good to anybody. But if you could find a way of draining away the water and making the ground solid, farmers could grow things on the dry earth. Okay, my idea is to build a big laser and use it to evaporate the water. No need to drain a marsh, then. You could just dry it out with the heat ray. Simple?''

Joe shook his head gloomily. ''Too simple. There's something wrong with it. I don't know what, but I'm sure it'll end in trouble.''

''Don't pay any attention to him,'' Irene said. ''It's a fine idea, Danny.''

''Suppose it sets fire to the whole countryside?" Joe grumbled. "Suppose it burns a hole right down to the center of the earth and starts a volcano?"

Danny winked at Irene. She nodded. Suddenly, they caught hold of Joe from each side and began tickling him unmercifully, in the ribs.

"Wait! Stop!" he yelled, squirming. "Cut it out! I can't—hee, hee, hee—stand it! Eek, ook, awk! Yow! No, no, no!"

He collapsed and fell to the sidewalk, and they let him alone. He finished laughing, sat up, and wiped his face.

"All right," he said. "If that's the way you want to answer intelligent scientific criticism—now, wait a minute. Don't tickle me any more, my stomach hurts from laughing. But seriously, how are you going to build a laser big enough to dry up Burton's Bog?"

"Oh, we won't. We'll use the Professor's laser," said Danny.

"But that's so small it won't dry up more than a square yard."

"A square yard is all we need. We'll take a couple of buckets of water and make a muddy patch in the garden, behind my house," Danny explained. "A kind of model marsh. It'll be enough to demonstrate how the idea will work."

They had reached Elm Street by now. Danny went on, "Let's hurry. I want to tell the Professor about it. There's no reason why he can't do it right now, this afternoon."

They ran across the street. Irene said, "Look how brown all the grass is, from the dryness. The Professor will have to be careful."

"He'll be careful." Danny stopped and sniffed. "I can smell smoke. I'll bet there's another forest fire up on the slopes of Sugarloaf. I wonder if Mr. Matthews is out flying?"

He went on to his own front gate, and the others followed him. But when they found Mrs. Dunn, who was ironing in the living room in front of the television set, she told them that the Professor had gone to Midston University for a very important conference with several faculty heads.

"He'll be back in time for dinner, I expect," she said. "You'll just have to be patient."

They tramped out to the kitchen and found some cookies and milk.

"I don't see why we have to be so patient," Danny said. "It's such a simple thing to do. If Mr. Pippit could just see it— Gosh, why shouldn't we do it ourselves? I wonder if Mr. Pippit is at his hotel?"

"Probably not," said Irene.

Danny scratched his chin thoughtfully. "Why don't you try him?" he said.

"Me? Try him? Why me?" Irene sat up straight, switching her pony tail over her shoulder.

"Because," Danny said, patiently, "if I get him on the phone he'll hang up as soon as he knows who it is. But you could find out if he's in and then go see him, and—well, you could be charming and glamorous and talk him into coming here. Girls are supposed to be able to do things like that, aren't they?"

"And you and Joe will sit here and eat cookies, I suppose, until I come back with Mr. Pippit following me like Mary's little lamb."

"Joe and I will get the ground properly wet," Danny answered, with dignity. "And we'll set up the laser and prepare the whole experiment."

"Maybe you don't know how to work the laser?" Joe said.

"Nothing to it. I watched the Professor. All he did was turn the power on when the voltage was reached. It isn't all that complicated a device."

"What if he won't come?" said Irene. "That is, if he's in, in the first place."

"Then we'll have a little mud in the yard,"

Danny said. "And the Professor can try him tomorrow. How about it, Irene?"

"All right. Where do you think he's staying?"

"Only one place he would stay," said Danny. "The Imperial Hotel. It's the fanciest place in town."

He got the phone book and looked up the number. Irene dialed, and asked for Mr. Pippit.

"They're ringing his room," she said to the others, covering the mouthpiece with her hand, "so this is where he's staying. But I'll bet he's not— Oh, hello. Mr. Pippit?"

They could hear his sharp voice, speaking tinnily.

"My name is Irene Miller, Mr. Pippit. I wonder if I could come and see you this afternoon? It's about Professor Bullfinch's machine, the laser— Oh, yes, it's *very* important—I'll explain that when I come—in fifteen minutes? Oh, yes, I can make it easily. Goodby."

She hung up and blew out a long breath. Then she tugged her skirt straight, tucked her blouse in smoothly, and patted her hair.

"I'll have to run all the way," she said. "I hope I have wind enough left to be glamorous. And you get that thing working—and don't be like Eddie. Test it, and make sure it doesn't fail."

"Don't worry," said Danny. "It'll be AOK."

Mr. Pippit had settled into the best suite of the Imperial Hotel, and the place already showed signs of his energetic personality. Clothing was scattered about from open suitcases as though he had had no time to hang anything up; there were newspapers, reports, scribbled notations, and file folders on every flat surface in both the rooms he occupied. A public stenographer sat with her pad ready in one corner. A second telephone had been installed. When Irene arrived, Mr. Pippit was pacing restlessly back and forth with one of the telephones in his hand. It had a long, trailing cord which he kept tripping over. At her knock, he jerked the door open and let her in, and then said, almost in one breath:

To Irene: "Come in. Be with you in a minute."

To the stenographer: " 'Will discuss the matter at length on that date.' Did you get that? Then go type it out."

To the telephone: "Don't argue, George. Can't stand argument. Want those proxies ready for the meeting on the fourth. Good-by."

He slammed down the phone and whirled to

inspect Irene. "What do you want? Got the wrong room?"

"No, sir. I don't think so, Mr. Pippit," Irene said, rather timidly. "I'm Irene Miller. I phoned you about an appointment."

Mr. Pippit snorted. "But you're a kid," he said. "Sounded like a woman on the phone. Thought you were Bullfinch's secretary."

"Well, I'm not," said Irene, beginning to feel a little snappish herself. "Do you want me to go? Or shall I tell you why I called?"

"Don't lose your temper," said Mr. Pippit. He pulled out a long cigar and lit it, peering at her over the match. "Bad for the digestion. Never lose *my* temper. Healthy as an ox. Sit down."

She took a chair. He clasped his hands behind his back and stuck his chin out at her. "Go ahead," he said. "Tell me what's on your mind."

"It's about Professor Bullfinch's laser. We've found a good use for it," Irene said.

"We? Who's we?"

Irene said, somewhat self-consciously, "Why—um—Danny and I."

"Danny? Dunn? I know him. Boy who led me through every cellar in Midston. Ruined my suit. Ran into my stomach. Ruined my lunch. Hmph! Don't want anything to do with him.''

At this, in spite of Mr. Pippit's warning, Irene did lose her temper. She shot up out of her chair and said angrily, "I think you care more about your old suit than you do about science or—or business, or *anything!* I thought important people like you didn't care how old a person was, as long as they had bright ideas. Danny's got a perfectly wonderful idea for using the laser. Somebody will understand it and—and make a lot of money with it. But it won't be you. You'll be too busy sneering at what you call *kids*.''

Mr. Pippit regarded her shrewdly. Then he waved his cigar at her. "Calm down," he said. "I remember what Bullfinch said about you and the boy. Interested in science. Thought scientists never flew off the handle.''

"I'm sorry," Irene said. "I didn't mean to fly off the handle, or yell, or get excited. But you keep talking about how practical you are— well, this is a practical idea. I'll tell you something. We almost had a fire in school today. The three grownups who were there didn't have sense enough to move, but Danny did—he put the fire out. That's practical, isn't it? He may be a boy, but he's got better ideas than some grownups.''

"Hmm." Mr. Pippit considered for a moment. Then he said, "What do you want me to do?"

"I want you to come and just *look* at Danny's demonstration for using the laser. It'll only take a few minutes."

"Where?"

"At Professor Bullfinch's house."

Mr. Pippit snapped his fingers. "I'll do it. Always act on impulse. That's how I get ahead. But I warn you—if it's some kid's trick, or foolishness, there'll be trouble. Well?"

"It's not foolishness. Do you want to go now?"

"Right now. No point in wasting time."

He snatched up an old tweed jacket and jammed his arms into the sleeves. Irene heaved a deep sigh, and then giggled.

"What's the matter?" said Mr. Pippit, raising his eyebrows. "Something wrong with my jacket? It's my favorite, even if it is an old one."

"Oh, no, it has nothing to do with your jacket," said Irene. "It's just that—well, I was thinking—I got you to come with me after all, but I—I wasn't very glamorous, was I?"

10
Mr. Pippit's
Hot Spot

Long before Mr. Pippit arrived, Danny and Joe had everything ready. They had chosen a bare patch of ground near the edge of the yard, far enough from any of the dry bushes or trees to avoid accidentally setting them on fire. Using a spade, they had scooped off the topsoil with its grass stalks, leaving a square of earth some three feet wide by five feet long, and they had brought water in pails and saturated it until it would hold no more. Its wet, brown, chocolate texture contrasted with the powdery ground all about it. They had two pails full of water ready to give it a final dousing when Mr. Pippit came.

Danny had brought out the laser, tested it on one corner of the wet patch, and found to his satisfaction that it worked as he had predicted. There was nothing left to do then but wait. Joe had no problem in this department: he curled up with his back against a tree, pulled out his notebook, and began murmuring, "laser, razor, glazer, gazer—" But Danny walked up and down biting his nails and wondering what to say to Mr. Pippit that would sound gentle and soothing.

At last the gleaming automobile rolled into the Professor's driveway. Irene hopped out, and as Danny hurried to meet her, she said, "No problems?"

Danny made a circle of his finger and thumb. "Not a one. Hello, Mr. Pippit. I'm glad you could come. Will you just step around to the back with us?"

"Very well," said Mr. Pippit. "Want to tell me what your idea is?"

"Yes, I'll explain in a minute."

"How come Bullfinch isn't in on this?" Mr. Pippit demanded. "Is he out of town?"

"Oh, no, he's busy at the university and I couldn't reach him. But I got this idea and it seemed like a good one, and I thought there wasn't any use wasting time—"

"Smart!" Mr. Pippit looked at Danny with sudden approval. "Boy after my own heart.

Like to jump into things myself, make quick decisions, carry 'em out.''

Joe, who was walking behind them, mumbled, "Oh, Danny has quite a reputation for headstrongery.''

"Eh? Headstrongery?'' said Mr. Pippit. "What kind of a word is that?''

"Kind of nice, isn't it?'' Joe said, proudly. "I just invented it. I also invented a motto for him: 'Leap before you look.' My own motto is, 'Sleep before you look.' ''

Mr. Pippit uttered a short laugh, as explosive as his way of talking.

When they came to the muddy patch, Dan emptied the two pails of water over it, and said, "Joe, will you and Irene please go and fill these again. We may need some more.''

They went off, and he motioned Mr. Pippit to stand beside him at the laser. He aimed the lens of the device at the muddy patch.

"Let's say that's a big marsh,'' he said. "If you could build a great big laser—and there's no reason why you couldn't if you could get a power source, big enough lights, and a big crystal—you could just dry up the marsh so that people could use the ground for planting or building. Like this.''

He threw the switch. The laser began to hiss

and its red beam shot out and touched the edge of the wet dirt. Its sound was drowned by a much louder hissing and sputtering. A cloud of steam arose. Danny moved the ray from side to side, and then shut it off.

"There!" he said. "Look at that."

The earth where the beam had played was nearly dry. Little curls of smoke lifted from its surface.

"Very ingenious," said Mr. Pippit. "Got to admit, you're pretty sharp. Only one trouble. Generally, a bog or marsh is formed by water seeping in from springs under the ground. Can't get at them to dry them up, not even with a laser, in most cases."

Danny's face fell. "Gosh, I never thought of that," he said.

"Mmm. Don't be too discouraged. Gives me another idea," snapped Mr. Pippit. "As long as Bullfinch isn't here— That thing heats up the ground, doesn't it?"

"Yes," said Danny.

"Turn it on again. Aim it at another wet patch."

Danny did so.

Mr. Pippit walked forward. He pointed to the spot where the beam was now striking. Steam was sizzling up once more. When the steam was gone, the ground began to glow.

"Aha! Thought so!" said Mr. Pippit. "Turns the stones red hot."

"But I don't see—" Danny began. He joined Mr. Pippit at the edge of the muddy patch, and watched the beam of the laser boring into the earth.

"Imagine this is enemy territory," said Mr. Pippit. "We've got the laser mounted in a plane. Let's say that's a fuel dump. First, burn holes in the gasoline supply drums."

"But, listen—" Danny protested.

Mr. Pippit paid no attention. He was seeing a battle before his eyes, and he began to get excited. "The gas goes up!" he cried. "Or suppose it's an airfield. We not only fry their planes, we melt the ground itself so that they can't take off or land!"

"But the Professor doesn't—" said Danny.

"We cook their roads. No transportation. Can't move!" Mr. Pippit exclaimed. He began to dance about, pointing first to one spot, then another. "A railroad station here. Melt the trains! A harbor over here. Focus on the water and boil the— OW!"

"What?" Danny said. "Boil the ow?"

Mr. Pippit was still dancing around. But he no longer looked cheerful and absorbed. His face was distorted and his mouth wide open. "Ow!" he yelled. "Yow! Help!"

"He's on fire!" Irene shrieked.

In his excitement, Mr. Pippit had moved directly in front of the laser's beam. Only for an instant—but that was enough to start his jacket charring. When he swung round, the smouldering patch burst into a blaze.

Danny ran to switch off the laser. It was to Joe's credit that this time he was alert and ready. He had been standing by with an extra pail of water. Almost before the words were out of Irene's mouth, he dashed the water over Mr. Pippit. Then he grabbed the second pail from Irene and threw that. In his eagerness, he made one slight mistake. He let go of the pail. It hit Mr. Pippit between the shoulders and

knocked him flat in the center of the muddy patch.

"Oops," said Joe automatically. "Sorry."

Irene darted from one side and Danny from the other. But before they could reach him, Mr. Pippit had pushed himself up and bounced back to his feet.

The three young people stared at him in horror. He was drenched from head to foot and stained with mud. There was a large burned spot on the back of his jacket, and a strong smell of charred tweed hung about him. His bulging eyes fairly snapped with fury.

He looked down at himself.

Then he said, "Another suit gone!"

He spun on his heel and strode away from them. He got into his car and slammed the door and drove away with a whirl of gravel under the wheels, leaving them still standing, petrified, like three statues with their mouths open.

11
Trouble with Fire

The Professor came home at about five o'clock. He parked his battered but stout-hearted old sedan in the driveway and went directly to his laboratory. He was feeling a little out of sorts; the faculty members at the meeting he had attended had reported very little success with Mr. Pippit. Mr. Pippit had a way of making even the mildest of them angry, and even though he had seemed impressed by most of the work being done in research, every meeting with him had ended in sharp words and raised voices. So far, he had not announced a decision either way about his grant to the university.

The Professor sat down and lit his pipe. He pulled a sheaf of notes out of his pocket and began to study them. Suddenly, he raised his head and listened. A gentle tap had sounded at the outer door.

"Is someone there?" he called. "Come in, whoever you are."

To his astonishment, it was Danny who opened the door and came in. It was so unlike the boy to knock—and especially so timidly—that Professor Bullfinch sat up straight and said, "Why, Dan, what on earth is the matter? Are you sick?"

Danny nodded silently, standing beside the Professor with his eyes lowered.

The Professor put down his pipe. "Perhaps I'd better call a doctor?"

"I'm not sick that way," said Danny.

"Oh?" Professor Bullfinch lifted his eyebrows thoughtfully, and sat back folding his hands over his stomach. "Care to tell me about it?"

"I *have* to tell you about it," said Danny. "That's why I'm sick."

He took a deep breath and plunged on. He told how he had had the idea of using the laser to dry up swamps, and how Irene had talked Mr. Pippit into coming to see it. And he described the unfortunate end to that promising demonstration. When he had finished, he took a deep breath and looked straight at Professor Bullfinch.

"I guess I just went ahead and acted without thinking again," he said. "I'm sorry. I try and try, but it's just something I can't help, like—like your smoking a pipe, I guess."

"Yes, Dan, I know," said the Professor soberly. "It's a fault, a serious fault." Then he slammed his hand on the papers on his desk so suddenly and loudly that Danny jumped. "But I'd rather you had a good, honest fault like that, than the kind of faults some adults have."

"Wh—what?" Danny stammered.

"Never mind," the Professor said. "As far as I can make out from your story, it was Pippit's own doing. He got carried away in his make-believe war, and jumped in front of the laser all by himself, without any help from you."

"But Joe—"

"Joe is a fine young man, a good poet, and an idiot," said the Professor affectionately. "I'm sure if Mr. Pippit stops to think about it he'll see that he was better off wet than with a neat little hole burned into him. Now, mind you, this doesn't mean I think you did well. You should have waited until I got home. You certainly should not have used the laser without consulting me. It is rather dangerous, as you have learned. I hope you will try to curb your impulses in the future.''

"Oh, I will, Professor," Danny said, with a sigh of relief.

Professor Bullfinch swiveled his chair around and reached for the phone. "I'm afraid you'll have to ask Mr. Pippit's pardon," he said. "From what I know of him, it may be a rather difficult job. But I don't see how you can escape it."

"No," Danny said. His shoulders sagged again. "But—but what'll I say? Gosh, I don't think he'll even talk to me."

"I'll see if I can persuade him to," said the Professor, dialing the number of the hotel. "Hello? Hotel Imperial? This is Professor Bullfinch. I'd like to speak to Mr. Glenway Pippit. What? He's *what?*"

The Professor leaped out of his chair, clutching the telephone. "When? I see. He did? Did he leave any message for me? No? Very well, thank you."

He hung up, and passed a hand over his bald head. "That's done it," he said.

"Done what? What happened?" Danny was hopping from one foot to the other, bursting with curiosity.

"He's gone," said the Professor. "Left the hotel about three minutes before I called.

Packed up, ordered his car brought round, cleared his things out, paid his bill, and drove off. He didn't leave any messages."

The telephone rang shrilly. The Professor snatched it up. "Yes?" he said. "Who? Oh, yes, Mr. Richards. Eh? Well, well, is that so? He said *what?* I see—No, I haven't any idea what he meant. Yes, well, I'll think it over. Perhaps there's something I can do. Oh, don't worry too much, something's bound to turn up. Good-by."

He turned away from the phone, shaking his head. "That was Mr. Richards calling from the university. He said he had a phone call from Mr. Pippit just a few minutes ago, and tried to call me about it but my line was busy. What a mix-up! Mr. Pippit announced that he was leaving town. Said he'd had enough of Midston. Said he couldn't afford to lose any more suits. Mr. Richards wanted to know if I had any idea what that meant. I didn't see any reason to get into a long discussion with him over the phone about your part in all this. Perhaps it's all for the best. Mr. Pippit was rather a difficult person to deal with, at best."

Danny was almost crying. "Oh, gosh, Professor!" he wailed. "You mean the university has lost that million dollars? And I'm to blame.

Oh, golly, I wish I'd never gone for that plane ride. I wish I'd never been born!''

The Professor put his hands on Danny's shoulders, and shook him gently. "Now, now, my boy," he said, "none of that. You're much too intelligent for that kind of nonsense. It would certainly be very convenient if we could put all the blame on you, and say that the whole thing was the fault of young Dan Dunn. It would make things very easy for me, and for all the other members of the science department of Midston. But the truth is, we've all had our run-ins with Mr. Pippit. I'm sure he felt we were too dreamy eyed and impractical for him. He was probably just looking for an excuse to break off the whole thing, and you and your friends furnished him with it."

Danny rubbed his nose on his sleeve. "Yes, I see that," he said. "Maybe you're right. But you'll have to tell Mr. Richards and the others sooner or later."

"We'll cross that bridge when we come to it," said the Professor. "Bless my soul! You startled me."

The last part of his speech was not intended for Danny. Irene had stuck her head in at the open window.

"Hi," she said. "I didn't mean to interrupt you. I—um—just wanted to—"

"I told him," Danny said.

"Oh. Well, the reason I came over," Irene went on, looking rather nervously at Professor Bullfinch, "was that I was just listening in on my short-wave radio and I heard something that—well, maybe it has something to do with—with what happened. I got a police broadcast telling Car something-or-other to be on the lookout for a blue Rolls Royce convertible which had gone through a police radar check-point at sixty miles an hour. They said it was believed the car had turned off Route 2 into one of the side roads leading north. Mr. Pippit had a—"

"—blue Rolls Royce convertible," Danny finished. "And we just heard the news that he's left town. Yeeks! Now he'll be arrested for speeding on top of everything else!"

"Well, that's what worries me," Irene said. "That he *won't* be arrested."

"Huh?" Both Danny and the Professor stared at her. "This is no time for joking." "Are you nuts?" They both spoke at the same time.

"Not at all. And I'm perfectly serious. You told me yourself, Danny, that Mr. Pippit is mad for short cuts."

"Sure. What of it?"

"I'm positive he turned north into Cowbridge Road, because that's the short cut leading from Route 2 northward and over to U.S. 1. You can see it on the map.''

"So what? Just because a man takes a short cut is no reason to want him arrested,'' said Danny. "And we're already in enough trouble with him.''

"Nothing like the trouble he'll be in if he did take Cowbridge Road. You know where Cowbridge Road runs?''

"Through the hills and along the far slopes of Rose Hill,'' Danny said.

"That's right. And just before I heard that police broadcast, I was listening to the reports of a new forest fire. Remember when you smelled smoke earlier this afternoon, Dan? Well, it's burning in the woods to the north, and by now the other end of Cowbridge Road may be cut off!''

12
"Fight Fire with Fire!"

For a long moment, neither Danny nor the Professor could speak. Then Professor Bullfinch exclaimed, "Great Jumping Jupiter! Are you sure?"

Irene nodded.

"But maybe he turned back before he got to the fire," said Danny.

"Maybe he did. But you know, when you get about two miles up Cowbridge Road there's an old logging road that turns off to the left? It looks like a good road, at first."

"Yes, it runs through the valley between Sugarloaf and Rose Hill. You mean, he might have turned back when he saw the fire. Then he might have tried that road, hoping it was another short cut?"

"That's right," said Irene. "But it isn't. It's a dead end."

The Professor started for the door. "I'm going after him," he said, grimly.

"No, wait, Professor," Irene said. "You might be trapped."

"I'll have to take that chance. I don't think there's that much danger, though. I think if I start this minute I can catch up with him before he gets into that logging road."

He was out the back door of the laboratory in six long strides. In spite of his plumpness, he could move rapidly when he wanted to, and he leaped into his car and was backing out of the driveway while Danny was still shouting after him, "Professor Bullfinch! Wait a minute!"

"Gosh," said Irene. "What'll we do now?"

"I don't know," Danny said. "I wish we could follow him."

"What good would that do?"

Danny beat his fist into his palm. "None, I guess. But I wish we could anyway. If only my mother was home, she could drive us after him in her car. But she went shopping after she finished her ironing, and she isn't back yet."

"I'll tell you what we can do," said Irene. "We can go over to my house and listen to the reports of the fire on my radio. Maybe we'll hear that everything's okay, now. Maybe they've stopped it from spreading.''

Danny followed her next door. Her radio was still on, and as they entered her room they heard a voice, crackling with static, saying, ''Al? This is Winston. The wind has died down, anyway. That's one good thing.''

''That's one of the firemen in a truck with a radio,'' Irene said. ''They keep reporting back to the fire chief.''

Another voice said, ''We're getting it under control in Sector Four.''

Still a third voice, which must have been that of the chief, said, ''Good work. Winston, this is Al again. Is she still spreading down toward Rose Hill?''

''Yeah—If we could just get up in there and start a backfire we could keep it from coming across the hills.''

''What does he mean?'' Irene asked.

''Oh, a backfire is when they start a fire themselves and burn off a strip of ground,'' Danny explained. ''Then the forest fire comes up to the burned strip and can't cross it, and that way they can keep it from spreading. But the wind has to be just right and you have to be able to control the backfire, see? That's what they mean when they say you can fight fire with fire. Since the wind has died down, now, they're thinking of trying it. Shh! I want to listen.''

"—chance of getting over the summit of Sugarloaf?" the chief was saying.

"There's no way of going around by the south," Winston replied. "Maybe you could send some guys down from Sector Four to climb Sugarloaf."

They heard some confused noises, and then the chief said, "—think we'll try. Wait a sec. What? Winston, there's a State trooper here who says he thinks two cars went up toward the logging road. They'd be cut off in there, by now. Did any of your men try that?"

"Not my men," Winston said. "Maybe Gus and his crew—"

Danny gripped Irene's wrist so hard that she winced. "It's Professor Bullfinch," he said. "And Mr. Pippit. I'll bet you anything you like."

Irene bit her lip. "What can we do?" she said. "There must be something—"

Danny snapped his fingers. "Fight fire with fire!" he cried. "I've got an idea. It's a long shot, but maybe it's worth trying."

Danny snatched up a pencil and one of the sheets of paper that were scattered about Irene's workbench. He began to draw a rough map.

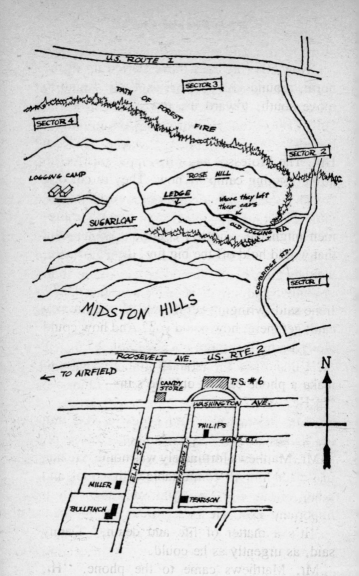

"Now, the fire must have started up in the north, around U.S. 1," he said. "It began to move south, toward us, toward the Midston Hills. They were talking about trying to set a backfire somewhere on the other side of Rose Hill. The Professor and Mr. Pippit must be up at the logging camp by now. They're cut off. But if I could get up over the summit of Sugarloaf, the way the chief was saying the firemen might go, and if I could start a backfire that would hold off the big fire, they'd be safe, wouldn't they?"

"Oh, Danny, how can you talk like that?" Irene said, wringing her hands. "If the firemen can't get there, how could you? And how could you possibly get there quickly enough?"

"I'll show you," he answered. "I've got to make a phone call. If only he's in—"

"He? Who?"

"Mr. Matthews!" And Danny darted into the hall, where the upstairs phone was kept.

Mr. Matthews fortunately was home. He had just made himself comfortable with a book and a cup of tea, and Mrs. Matthews said, "Is it important, Dan? He's very tired."

"It's a matter of life and death," Danny said, as urgently as he could.

Mr. Matthews came to the phone. "Hi,

109

Dan,'' he said. ''More problems about how a plane flies?''

''No, sir. You've got to help me, you've just *got* to.''

''Help you? Sure. What do you want to know?''

''It's nothing like that. The Professor—he's in danger.''

''Huh?'' Mr. Matthews was silent for a second, and then he said, ''Now, listen, Danny, maybe you'd better—''

''No, *you* listen. He drove off to get Mr. Pippit, who left town a while ago. They're both up in the hills. They've been trapped by the forest fire.''

''The forest fire? How do you know?''

''We've been listening to the reports on short wave. Now if we could get up above Sugarloaf, near where the old logging camp is—you know the spot I mean, don't you?—and start a backfire, we could keep the main fire from spreading so that he and Mr. Pippit would have a chance to escape.''

There was another pause, a longer one. Then Mr. Matthews said, ''Get up above Sugarloaf? I don't see how—''

''You could fly me up there,'' said Danny.

''Fly? You're off your rocker, son. Even if

I did fly you there, we couldn't land. Not in the hills, not with a fire raging.''

"You wouldn't have to land. I could start a backfire from the plane, with the laser.''

"You could start a backfire from the plane with the laser. Sure, I see," Mr. Matthews repeated. "WHAT? What's a laser?''

"Oh, I forgot, you don't know about it. It's a heat ray.''

"Ha, ha, ha!" laughed Mr. Matthews. "It sounded just like you said *heat ray*.''

"I did say heat ray. That's what it is. The Professor developed it. That's one of the reasons Mr. Pippit came to Midston. It's—it's one of the reasons he left, too. It's a beam that can start a fire at a distance.''

He could hear Mr. Matthews mumbling, "Oh, boy! Now I've heard everything. I've flipped my wig, that's what's happened. I *must* be crazy to be listening to this. You want me to fly you up over Sugarloaf, near where the forest fire is burning, so that you can start a backfire with a magical heat ray. Is that it?''

"Mr. Matthews," said Danny, as earnestly as he could, "you've got to believe me. I know this is a risk. I know it's a big chance to take. But I'm sure it will work. I can't go to the police or the fire department, because they wouldn't listen to a boy. But you know me, and you know the Professor. The laser really exists, and it isn't magical. It's a scientific invention. If anything happened to the Professor, and you found out later that I was right and that you hadn't done anything about it, just think how you'd feel.''

When Mr. Matthews spoke again, it was in an altered voice. ''Okay,'' he said. ''You're right. Look, is your mother there?''

''No. I don't know where she is. She went shopping, but—''

''She's probably out with half the rest of the town, looking at the smoke. Have you got that laser, or whatever it is, there now?''

''Yes.''

''All right, get it out on the sidewalk in front of your house. I'll drive over and I'll pick you up in five minutes. I'm leaving now!''

13
A Message in the Rock

The little red Piper Colt bobbed and bumped in the currents of hot air caused by the fire, as if it were a small car on a bad dirt road. The whole sky was a dirty gray; the sun was hidden in a haze of smoke so that it looked like a pale yellow ball. Around the horizon in a great crescent that stretched from the northwest to the southeast was a line of thick smoke in which, here and there, orange flames licked up, clearly visible against the dark ground and the dark cloud. The air was full of the smell of burning wood, and flakes of ash drifted past the windshield of the airplane. They were flying toward Sugarloaf, so low that they could plainly see the scraggly blueberry bushes on its stony summit. Beyond it, across the valley, was Rose Hill. And there, where the gray line of a dusty road ran, the trees and bushes were burning with a sound like the crumpling of an immense sheet of cellophane, or the popping and snapping of a giant bowl of breakfast cereal. That part of the fire was still a good distance off, to the east and south, but they could see that the road vanished into it so that no one could pass that way.

"Wow!" Danny breathed. "Some fire."

"How do I get myself into these things?" Mr. Matthews pretended to groan, and shook his head. "Oh, well, at least we have a good view. I'm going to fly over Sugarloaf and turn a bit north to spot the old logging camp."

"Okay. And I'll keep an eye out for the Professor," said Danny.

Sugarloaf passed beneath them; then they were over a wide valley, thickly wooded.

"I can see the track of the logging road," Danny said.

"You're going to have trouble spotting those two men down there among the trees," said Mr. Matthews.

"I know," Danny answered. "But I'm hoping if they're stuck somewhere, they'll come out in the open when they hear the plane and try to signal to us. Look! There's the logging camp."

The woods had opened out, and in a clearing below appeared a light gray oblong—the roof of a weathered shed which had once been a sawmill. Danny and Mr. Matthews peered down until their eyes watered from the effort, but there was no sign of the two men or their cars.

"What now?" said Mr. Matthews.

Danny had been certain he would see them, and he could barely hide his disappointment. But he had planned out the next move in advance.

"The other side of Rose Hill is grassy," he said. "There are very few trees—mostly blueberry and bayberry bushes, and some wild roses. I'm sure that's what the fire chief was talking about when he mentioned setting a backfire. If you can swing around and fly along that slope, I'll get the laser ready."

The airplane droned in a sweeping half-circle, over the clearing. Mr. Matthews flew east a little way until they were approaching the smooth flanks of Rose Hill. It was not as high as Sugarloaf, but a good deal longer. They were closer to the edge of the fire here; it came crackling down from the north through the woods, sending up greenish-white and dark

gray billows through which they glimpsed the
burned-out patches beyond. On the southern
side, where the hill dropped away, there was
a thin line of smoke that cut across the far end
of the logging road. But closer at hand, the fire
still had half a mile or so to go before it reached
the slopes.

Danny had wrestled the laser into his lap, its
cable stretching over his shoulder to the port-
able power source, which had been stored behind his seat. He slid open the window on his
side, and propped the laser up so that its nozzle
rested on the sill.

"I think we've got a good chance," he
yelled over the noise of the motors and the air
whistling past his face. "Look at the smoke.
There's a wind now—and it's blowing away
from the hill, toward the main fire."

He snapped the switch. The red beam, almost invisible in the daylight, stabbed downward. Danny held his breath.

Suddenly a bright spot flared out far below,
on the hillside. Flames shot up from the dry
grass. As the plane flew along above the slope
it seemed to be drawing a line with a tremen-
dously long thin pencil, a line of bright fire.

Danny shut off the laser. Almost at the same
moment, the ground seemed to fall away from

him and he had the sensation of spinning around and standing on his ear. It only lasted for a minute; then things returned to normal.

"Sorry if I startled you," Mr. Matthews said. "I had to pull up and away. We were getting too close to the fire down at the southern end of the hills."

He had swung the plane around again. The line of flame they had started, helped by the breeze, had swept down the whole side of Rose Hill. A broad black band showed where it had burned away the grass.

"That ought to make a good firebreak," Danny said, closing his window. "Anyway, everything on this side of Rose Hill should be safe, now. The fire can't jump that burned-out strip."

"Good work," said Mr. Matthews. "Say, isn't that the famous Rolls Royce?"

Danny looked down. They were flying back over the logging road again, somewhat higher this time. And there, its creamy leather upholstery and shiny blue sides making it stand out, was Mr. Pippit's automobile. It had been left in an open space off the road. After a moment, Danny could make out the darker shape of the Professor's old sedan close by.

"They must have parked the cars and set out

on foot when they saw they were cut off," said Mr. Matthews. "Question is, where are they now?"

"They certainly didn't go up Rose Hill," said Danny. "I'll bet Mr. Pippit drove up the road and found it ended at the logging camp. Then the Professor caught up with him. They came back here and saw they couldn't drive through. They must have started to climb the foothills, hoping to get up on Sugarloaf."

"Mmhmm." Mr. Matthews shook his head, sadly. "I hope I have enough gas left to search the whole territory. Otherwise, we may have to climb Sugarloaf ourselves."

He guided the airplane in a wide loop over the whole mass of hills. As he came back up from the south once more, the plane bumped violently. The fire had crept into the rocky foothills of Sugarloaf, leaping from one tree to another. They could see the tall, dark trunks wrapped in flame, and here and there glowing pockets among the rocks where bushes were burning.

Then they both saw it at the same time—a small white patch waving back and forth. Danny grabbed Mr. Matthews' arm.

"Don't *do* that, friend," said Mr. Matthews. "Not while I'm flying this crate."

"I'm sorry. But it's the Professor. See? He's

on that rocky shelf. He's waving his handkerchief, or something, tied to a stick like a flag.''

"I see him. There's Pippit, too. Sit tight.
I'll bank and make a pass in front of them so
we can see what they're up to."

The two men were standing on a broad ledge
to which they must have climbed to escape the
fire. Behind them rose a wall of solid limestone, smooth and bulging. On one side, the
ledge, rounding a corner, dropped away in a
mass of gravel into a wooded gorge from which
flames were rising in places. On the other side,
the shelf narrowed and vanished in a haze of
smoke.

Danny and Mr. Matthews took all this in as
the plane sped past.

"They're boxed in," said Mr. Matthews.

But Danny's eyes were sharper. "Not alto-
gether," he said. "It probably looks that way
to them, but on the left, where the ledge nar-
rows, there's a trail among the rocks. It leads
up toward the summit and then branches down
on the other side of the hill. I know this neigh-
borhood. I've climbed around Sugarloaf for
years."

"But there was smoke over that whole section of the ledge," Mr. Matthews protested.

"No, that's the way it looked, but there are
only a few bushes burning there. They could

Then they saw it at the same time—

a small white patch waving back and forth.

run past and be in the clear. Then they could climb up and get away safely. If we could only tell them—"

"That's just peachy," said Mr. Matthews. "What'll we do—send them a letter?"

"If I could yell to them to go to the left," Danny said, "do you think they'd hear me?"

"Not over the noise of the engine. Isn't there some other way of signaling?"

"Have you got a flashlight in here?"

"No. I ought to have, but I keep forgetting it. Anyway, how would you signal? With Morse code? I'll bet the Professor doesn't know any more Morse than I do. Most people don't."

"I guess you're right," Danny said, glumly. "But gosh, we can't just leave them there. When that rock gets hot—"

"I'll fly back and try to contact the fire department," said Mr. Matthews decisively. "They can lower a rope from the cliffs above, perhaps."

"Wait a second." Danny's eyes were sparkling. "We *can* signal to them. It'll be tricky, but I think we can do it."

"How?"

"With the laser. I thought of it just now when I said that the rock would get hot."

"You mean blink it on and off at them? But

we just agreed that Morse code wouldn't be of any use.''

''Not that kind of message. I'll use it to make a big arrow in the rock, pointing the way they should go.''

''Hmm. That's an interesting idea, son.'' Mr. Matthews scratched his chin. ''We'll have to be careful you don't miss or you'll burn your arrow right into their shirt fronts.''

''That rock wall is pretty high—''

''Yes, and the air is pretty bumpy. Look, I'll fly past as close as I can get to the ledge. You just make sure your seat belt is good and tight so that you don't go sailing out the window, laser and all. Okay. Ready? Here we go!''

He swung the plane away from the ledge and out in a wide swoop. Danny pushed back the window and readied the laser.

Mr. Matthews' jaw was set firmly. He flew straight along the face of the limestone wall. The engine seemed to roar more loudly. He came so close that it seemed his wing-tip would brush the stone and the plane would go crashing down to ruin.

Danny gripped the laser. He saw the pale limestone flash by, and the faces of Professor Bullfinch and Mr. Pippit, their mouths wide open, before they threw themselves down upon the ledge in fright. But he kept his head. He snapped on the machine and kept it steadily focused on the rock, and then he snapped it off in time. Chips flew, where the beam touched.

When the plane had flown out and around in its second sweep, they could both see, standing out sharply, a long, dark line cut in the limestone, pocked and pitted in places and looking as though a hot iron had been scraped along the wall.

Once again, Mr. Matthews made that breathtaking dash along the face of the cliff and only yards away from it. Once again, Danny snapped on the laser. This time, he made a short, angled stroke at one end of the line. Then a third time, and he had burned in the third stroke. The marks stood out bold and clear along the wall: an arrow pointing to the left.

The two men, unable to guess why the plane had flashed past so closely and nearly startled out of their wits, had dropped flat for safety. But the Professor had seen the faint glow of the laser's beam, and he had heard the popping and spitting of it as it hit the stone above him. Danny could see him jump to his feet and look upward. He grabbed Mr. Pippit's arm and pointed. They seemed to be arguing. Then the Professor caught up the stick with his handkerchief tied to it, and waved it.

The marks stood out bold and clear along the wall.

"He understands," Danny said, with relief.

With the Professor in the lead, the two men ran to the left end of the ledge. As the plane circled, Danny saw the Professor dart forward and vanish into the smoke. Mr. Pippit followed. A moment later, they reappeared higher up on the cliff. They paused for an instant to wave once more at the plane, and then they began the climb upward to safety.

14
"If I Only Had a Laser"

The greatest exhibition of courage, that day, was probably shown by Mrs. Dunn.

First, she had come home from her shopping late—she had stopped on Washington Avenue to chat with neighbors and stare anxiously at the veil of smoke that hung over half the sky— and had found Irene waiting for her with the news that the Professor and Mr. Pippit appeared to be marooned somewhere in the area of the forest fire, and that her son, Danny, was at that moment flying over it with her cousin, Mr. Matthews.

Mrs. Dunn was a woman of admirable calm and fortitude. She said to Irene, "In that case, I'd better set the table, because when they all get home they're going to be hungry."

Irene said, "But—but aren't you worried? They're in danger."

Mrs. Dunn smiled gently. "Of course I'm worried, dear," she replied. "But mothers have to get used to being worried. And there's nothing I can do about it. I prefer to keep busy, rather than run around screaming hysterically. It has been my experience that when men have been in danger they generally want refreshment. I may as well prepare for that."

"I'll stay here and help you," Irene said. "I'd rather keep busy, too."

She ran home to ask permission, and soon returned with her mother, who brought with her half a baked ham. "I thought this might help out," said Mrs. Miller. "Oh, dear, you must be so upset about Danny—and the poor Professor—I know I am—I can't just go home and wait there, so I'll wait here with you and help you set the table. If you don't mind, that is."

"Not at all," said Mrs. Dunn, cheerily. "You and Irene put out plates and silverware— you know where it is, dear, don't you?—and I'll start the coffee. And we can all worry together. But what about your husband?"

"Oh, he's listening to the radio. He'll be over with a report on the news if there's anything to tell."

It was past nine o'clock when Danny and the Professor came home at last. With them they brought Mr. Pippit, and Mr. and Mrs. Matthews. Irene ran home and got her father, and then they all sat down around the table together and attacked the cold meats and cheese and bread and butter and homemade biscuits and honey and jam and scrambled eggs and angel cake and pickles, all washed down by quarts of hot cocoa and coffee. They all talked too loudly and laughed too heartily, as people will who have been under a great deal of strain. Nobody minded elbows on the table or scattered crumbs. They all tried to talk at the same time, to explain to each other what had happened from the beginning. There was much interrupting of each other and cries of, "Well, while *you* were doing that, *we* were—" and so forth. Irene had phoned Joe to tell him the news, and midway through the meal he burst in and had to be brought up to date. And then, although he had had his dinner he had to be fed to revive him because, as he said, he felt quite faint from all the excitement.

"One of the best things," said the Professor, when the noise had subsided a little and Mrs. Dunn and Mrs. Miller began to clear some of the dishes away, "was the fact that the backfire Danny set on Rose Hill helped the firemen get the whole blaze under control. The chief was very complimentary, although I'm afraid he still doesn't understand exactly how it was done. But that big burned-out section kept the fire from spreading over the hills. A party of firemen had been sent to climb Sugarloaf and we met them and led them back to the southern foothills, where we'd been trapped. The fire hadn't really taken hold there, and they were able to put it out. Meanwhile, the men who had been further north, in what they called Sector Four, had gotten that part under control and were able to come down and manage the rest of the fire. By the time we left, the chief said the danger was over.''

"Their cars weren't badly harmed, either,'' said Mr. Matthews. "Except that I'm afraid Mr. Pippit's upholstery will smell of smoke for a while. But that's a small price to pay, I guess.''

"There's another good result,'' Mr. Pippit said, taking out his cigar case and offering it to the other men. "Had a long talk with Bull- finch out there while we were climbing around. Got me to see I'd been a fool. Don't mind admitting it. Always admit when I'm wrong, and try to do something about it.''

He held a match to his cigar and blew out

a plume of fragrant smoke. "Had to agree that theoretical stuff had to come first. Had to agree I was pigheaded. Talked it all over. Grateful to Danny, too, for saving our lives. Decided to give Midston the grant for the Research Center."

"That's very gratifying news, Mr. Pippit," said Dr. Miller, Irene's father. As an astronomer teaching at Midston, he had had his own brush with Mr. Pippit, and had been concerned about the Research Center. "I'm sure Mr. Richards will be delighted to hear it."

"Tell him in the morning," said Mr. Pippit. "Want to get some rest, now. Thought I'd go back to the hotel."

"There's no need to do that," Mrs. Dunn said. "We have plenty of room here. Heavens, I don't see any reason for you to pay the terrible prices the Imperial charges when you can stay here for nothing. And you'll be much more comfortable, too."

Mr. Pippit regarded her with respect and admiration. "Really want me, do you?" he said.

"Of course we do."

"Ma'am," he said, "I'd like nothing better. Best dinner I've had since I've been in Midston. And you're right, the hotel was too dratted expensive. Besides—" He cleared his throat, stared thoughtfully at his cigar, and then said firmly, "I was *lonely,* there. Glad to accept your invitation."

"And I promise I won't do anything sudden," Danny said, in a small voice.

Mr. Pippit grinned widely, looking more than ever like an enormous bullfrog.

"Well," Joe said, "I've got to go. I promised Mom I'd come right home. But before I do, I—um—it's sort of partly my fault that all this happened. I mean, if I had just held on to the bucket and let the water fly—"

"Forget it," said Mr. Pippit. "Glad you put me out."

"Thanks. Well, to sort of make up for hitting you with the bucket, I've—I've dedicated my poem to you," Joe said.

Mr. Pippit sat bolt upright. "Eh? Poem?" he said. "To me?"

"I hope you don't mind," said Joe.

A most extraordinary look spread over Mr. Pippit's face, an expression in which astonishment, pleasure, and embarrassment were blended. He grew very red. "Mind?" he said, at last. "First time it ever happened to me. Ridiculous. Don't know what to say. Mind? Certainly not. Very pleased."

"Fine. Then I'll recite it to you," said Joe.

And fixing his eyes on the ceiling, he began:

If I only had a laser
I'd be happy as a fish;
I would never need a razor,
I would melt my beard off—swish!

"Of course," he added, as an aside, "I haven't got a beard yet, and a fish isn't terribly happy, but this is what we poets call poetic license."

"Go on," said the Professor, vastly amused.

If I had a laser handy
I would weed my garden so,
Work would be as sweet as candy
And I'd never need a hoe.

In the woods in brisk November
I would warm my chilly toes,
I would use it in December
As a shovel when it snows.

To be neat and clean I'd choose it
For to empty out my pockets;
Independence Day I'd use it
On the fuses of my rockets.

I'd make kindling out of some trees,
Or I'd steam a tasty clam;
I could turn it on the plum trees,
and boil myself some jam.

But for school it's not the right beam,
'Cause I'm the kind of creature
Who'd forget it's not a light beam—
And shine it on the teacher!

Everyone applauded. "Well, Pippit, you ought to be very happy with that," laughed the Professor. "You wanted some practical applications, and Joe has given you a big handful of them."

Mr. Pippit stood up. With a solemn expression, he said slowly, "It is an excellent poem and shows great talent, and I am proud and happy to have had it dedicated to me."

This was the longest sentence anyone had ever heard him say, and they were all stunned. Then abruptly he barked, "Ought to give a grant for a Poetry Center. Think about it."

Joe, with a wide smile, began to say something.

"But not today," Mr. Pippit added. "Let's face it. Not practical enough."

The Professor pushed back his chair. "Isn't that someone knocking at the front door?"

"I'll go, Professor," said Mrs. Dunn, hurrying out.

The Professor beamed around the table. "I just want to say one more thing," he said. "Sometimes, we only learn by facing dangers.

134

But now, we're all happily gathered together here, and I am glad matters worked out well and we're all safe. Our troubles are over at last—"

He checked himself, looking inquiringly at the dining room door. A policeman stood there.

"Mr. Glenway Pippit?" the policeman said.

"That's me," said Mr. Pippit.

"Is that your car out in front, sir, the blue Rolls convertible?" asked the policeman.

"Yes, it is. Is it parked in the wrong place? Or what?"

"Oh, no, you're parked all right. We've been looking for you, Mr. Pippit. I've got something for you."

"Ah, a message?"

"No, sir," said the policeman, with a sigh. "A summons for speeding."

15
Snitcher's Plot

Miss Arnold looked with satisfaction at the exhibits for the Science Fair which were being lined up on a long table under the blackboard. Ronnie Greenfield had set up a display showing the life history of the butterfly, the Gianninoto twins had a large model of an atomic power plant they had made, and Victoria Williams and her friend Robin Glenn had prepared a demonstration on the making of a telescope. Some of the other pupils were carrying in their displays from the hallway.

"This is a splendid beginning," Miss Arnold said.

The school principal, Mr. Standish, stuck his head into the room. "May we come in?" he said. "I have a distinguished visitor with me today. Please come this way, Mr. Pippit."

Mr. Pippit followed him in, shook hands with Miss Arnold, and winked at Irene who was standing nearby.

"Can't stay long," he snapped. "Promised some friends I'd drop in for a minute and see the displays. Might be some ideas I can use. Always on the lookout for new young talent."

"Mr. Pippit is the gentleman I told you about," Mr. Standish said to Miss Arnold. "He is founding a Research Center at Midston."

"Oh, yes. We're glad to have you with us, Mr. Pippit," said Miss Arnold. "I'm very proud of this class. We have some fine young scientists here. And this is only the start. By next month, we expect to have at least a dozen more entries for the fair."

Danny and Joe brought in the wind tunnel and placed it on a table near the window. They had already greeted Mr. Pippit in the hall, and Danny said, "I hope you can stay long enough to watch the demonstrations and listen to the talks, sir."

"Going to have any demonstrations of poetry?" Mr. Pippit said.

Joe grinned. "Maybe I can sneak in a quick reading."

At the back of the classroom, Eddie Philips nudged his friend George Bessel. "Just wait," he whispered. "That smart-aleck Danny is going to get the surprise of his life."

"What'd you do?" George asked.

Eddie snickered. "Remember, when class started and all the displays were still out in the hall, I got permission to leave the room for a minute?"

"Yeah. I remember."

"I stopped at Danny's wind tunnel and made a little improvement in the electric fan."

"Improvement?" George looked blankly at Eddie.

"Uh-huh. The blade is held on the shaft by a setscrew. I unscrewed that and took the blade off, and put it on again backward. With the guard covering it nobody will notice anything wrong until he starts the fan."

"What'll happen?" said George.

Eddie looked at him in disgust. "Don't you know *anything?* Instead of pushing the air, it'll *pull* it. Instead of blowing smoke it'll suck it into the room, and the place will be full of it. Then we'll see what happens to Mr. Wise Guy Dunn."

All the displays were in, by now, and Miss Arnold clapped her hands for attention. "If you'll take your seats," she said, "we can start. Mr. Standish, you and Mr. Pippit can sit up here in front of my desk. Danny, suppose you make your announcement first.''

"Yes ma'am.'' Danny stood up in front of the class. "Well, as some of you know there was a kind of mix-up. Irene and Joe and I made this wind tunnel. It was supposed to be our display. And Sni—Eddie Philips made one, too. Only his got sort of smashed up and wrecked—''

Some of the pupils giggled. Danny's expression, however, remained solemn.

"Since then, we talked it over—I mean, Irene and I did,'' he went on. "We've decided that we're going to make a display showing a new device called a laser. We're going to explain how it works, and how its beam is different from an ordinary beam of reflected light.'' He paused and glanced at Eddie with a wicked smile. "And so we thought we'd give this wind tunnel, which is all finished and ready to go, to Eddie, to take the place of his. Here you are. It's all yours.''

Eddie sat motionless with a stupefied look on his face.

Miss Arnold said, "I think this is a very generous act on the part of Irene and Danny, considering all the work they have put into this project—''

"And Joe," said Joe, under his breath.

"When they told me about their decision, I thought we'd make it a little surprise. Now, Eddie, you may come up and demonstrate how the wind tunnel works."

Eddie got slowly to his feet, looking long-ingly at the door as if he wished he could make a dash for it. "I—I—" he stammered.

"Well, come along," said Miss Arnold. "I know you're surprised, and I'm sure you must be grateful. I know you want to thank Danny and Irene—"

"And Joe," mumbled Joe.

"Yeah. Sure. Thanks," said Eddie. Moving like someone wading in a swift stream, he ad-vanced to the front of the room. "Do I have to work the thing?" he said, desperately. "Maybe it doesn't work the same way mine did."

"It's the same idea," said Danny. "Only the smoke part is different. You see, we were going to use hydrochloric acid and ammonia fumes for the smoke, but then we figured that might be dangerous so we got one of those Fourth of July smokepots that makes colored smoke. It's all ready. You just start the fan. I'll light the smokepot. You know what will happen—I explained the whole thing to you, didn't I?"

"Yeah. I know what will happen," said Eddie, miserably.

He stood helplessly with his hand on the fan switch. "I—I don't feel so well," he muttered.

"Go on, Eddie," said Miss Arnold, firmly. "You're wasting time."

Danny had touched a match to the fuse of the smokepot. Eddie shut his eyes and snapped the switch. And at the same instant, he hurled himself backward, out of the way.

Mr. Pippit had risen to his feet, the better to see the demonstration. Eddie crashed into him and they both fell back across Miss Arnold's desk. There was a wild scramble for a moment, and then Mr. Standish pulled Eddie off and helped Mr. Pippit up.

"What on earth is the matter with you, Eddie?" cried Miss Arnold.

"Uh—uh—" Eddie stared at the wind tunnel. Danny stood beside it with an innocent air. The fan was blowing the smoke through the box, and out the partly opened window. Inside the box, the class could see the handsome model of an airplane wing rising on the air current, which was clearly marked by the stream of colored smoke flowing gently around it.

"Maybe he was afraid I didn't test the model carefully," Danny said, keeping a straight face. "But you see, I always check and double-check my experiments, Eddie. And I did check over this equipment, including the electric fan, *very* carefully before I brought it into the room. Somehow, the fan-blade got turned around. But it doesn't matter, because as long as it's moving in the same direction, the air will keep flowing in the same direction. It flows a little

more slowly, that's all, and that was a good thing for this model. So you see, there was nothing to worry about."

Joe gave a loud groan. "No? That's what you think," he said. He pointed at Mr. Pippit.

In the fall, Miss Arnold's inkwell had been

142

knocked over. Mr. Pippit's jacket now had a large, dripping, blue blotch on its front.

He glanced down at it. "Again?" he howled. "Another suit!"

Then he gave a shrug. "Getting to be a habit," he said. "May as well get used to it."

He sat down, again. "Never mind. Keep going," he said. "I've got lots of suits."

Danny looked at him in admiration. "Gee, Mr. Pippit," he breathed, "you sure have changed."

He picked up the pointer and handed it to Eddie. "Go on with the demonstration," he said, and he walked down the aisle to his seat with a grin that stretched from ear to ear.

ABOUT THE AUTHORS
AND ILLUSTRATOR

JAY WILLIAMS has written over twenty-five fiction and nonfiction books for children of all ages, in addition to coauthoring fifteen books about Danny Dunn. Mr. Williams was born in Buffalo, New York, and educated at the University of Pennsylvania, Columbia University, and the Art Students' League.

RAYMOND ABRASHKIN wrote and coproduced the very popular and successful "Little Fugitive," a film that won an award at the Venice Film Festival.

OWEN KAMPEN was born in Madison, Wisconsin. He attended the University of Wisconsin and for several years studied at the Art Students' League. During World War II, he was a B-24 pilot stationed in Italy. Mr. Kampen is a free-lance illustrator and a portrait painter.

29990 THE GREATEST MONSTERS IN THE WORLD, by Daniel Cohen. Illustrated with reproductions and photographs. The intriguing pros and cons of the existence of Bigfoot, Nessie, the Yeti, and many other possible and impossible monsters. ($1.50)

29802 SEA MONSTERS, written and illustrated by Walter Buehr. A fascinating discussion of the myths, facts, and scientific theories about the existence of giant sea creatures from prehistoric times to the present. ($1.25)

29953 GREAT MONSTERS OF THE MOVIES, by Edward Edelson. Illustrated with stills from the films. This survey of one of the most popular scary entertainments in this century covers the legends behind the stories and the brilliant directors and actors who created some of the most successful horror films. ($1.50)

29749 GREAT SCIENCE FICTION FROM THE MOVIES, by Edward Edelson. Illustrated with stills. This entertaining history reveals the intriguing combination of scientific fact and writers' imagination that has produced some of the most thought-provoking, strange, and exciting films of the twentieth century. ($1.25)

29998 STAR KA'AT, by Andre Norton and Dorothy Madlee. Illustrated by Bernard Colonna. An exciting rescue mission from outer space opens the way for a special friendship between two super-cats and two courageous kids. ($1.50)

29817 FOG MAGIC, by Julia L. Sauer. Illustrated by Lynd Ward. When Greta walks through the fog, she starts off on an adventure that takes her back to the past of one hundred years ago. ($1.25)

29948 BASIL OF BAKER STREET, by Eve Titus. Illustrated by Paul Galdone. The Mystery of the Missing Twins was one of the strangest and most baffling cases in the famous career of Basil— Sherlock Holmes of the mouse world. ($1.50)

29866 BASIL AND THE PYGMY CATS, by Eve Titus. Illustrated by Paul Galdone. Follow Basil to the mysterious East in one of the most perplexing cases of his famed career as the Sherlock Holmes of the mouse community. ($1.25)

(If your bookseller does not have the titles you want, you may order them by sending the retail price, plus 50¢ for postage and handling, to: Mail Service Department, POCKET BOOKS, a Simon & Schuster Division of Gulf & Western Corporation, 1230 Avenue of the Americas, New York, N. Y. 10020. Please enclose check or money order—do not send cash.)